DARKANSAS

DARKANSAS

A NOVEL

JARRET MIDDLETON

DZANC
BOOKS

DZANC BOOKS

5220 Dexter Ann Arbor Rd.
Ann Arbor, MI 48103
www.dzancbooks.org

Library of Congress Cataloging-in-Publication Data

Names: Middleton, J. R. D., 1985- author.
Title: Darkansas / Jarret Middleton.
Description: Ann Arbor, MI : Dzanc Books, [2017]
Identifiers: LCCN 2017003741 | ISBN 9781945814297
Subjects: LCSH: Family secrets--Fiction. | Twin brothers--Fiction.
Classification: LCC PS3613.I359 D37 2017 | DDC 813/.6--dc23
LC record available at https://lccn.loc.gov/2017003741

First US edition: August 2017
Interior design by Michelle Dotter

Printed in the United States of America

10   9   8   7   6   5   4   3   2   1

For my brother, Brett,
and for Rachel, always.

Blood a necklace on me all my life.
—Michael Ondaatje, *The Collected Works*
of Billy the Kid

The fact is
gods love to be honored by men.
—Euripides, *Hippolytos*

COLD CELESTIAL SKY OPENED *above the wilds of a long forgotten grove. Several sylvan acres away lay an awkward bit of Ozarks land fit for farming and raising up a hearty clan named Bayne. Occupiers of the property for every hard year of two or so hundred, they came to be put in that ground for every reason that existed for dying.*

Not long after its bloody inception, that place began to fade with the wear of time. A canopy of trees smothered the grove within its shade and separated it from the farthest reaches of the house, the road, and the surrounding county. Sugar maple, pine, oak, and elm grew strong against a meridian of tall grass. Tanglebrush and bramble spread across depressions and hills cut by jags of chert and barren plateaus of rock. The natural world thrived for most of a lifetime. That was, until the call of a culling warmed the soil.

Each generation, a peculiar moon would rise. Ethereal women lurked in the waves of overgrowth, beating it back into rows, scythes raised as they tended their special crop. Long black dresses covered their bodies and bonnets concealed their pale faces, each carrying an oblong sack hung down her back. The grove not only grew in its recess upon the earth but it spread back and forth in time, glowing at the hour of its harvest, the shadows of the solemn women cast against the surrounding wall of trees.

Jordan Bayne stepped out of the dark forest into the bounds of the grove. When his foot touched down in the soft vegetation, an alarm sounded in all directions. A blinding spotlight accompanied the pulsing siren. He could not see beyond the pale light but felt the whispering panic of the field maids. Those closest raised their heads and pinned Jordan beneath long stares. The women shuffled down the rows until they converged in groups that came straight toward him.

Jordan turned to run back into the trees but his body moved heavy and slow. They kept gaining. He tripped in a gulley and turned over on his back. A horde of grim faces with burning black eyes closed in until Jordan was eclipsed by the tapestry of their habits. Then, in unison, the figments of night raised their scythes and brought their blades down upon him.

ONE

THE DREAM ENDED AND Jordan's face creased with pain. A heavy blue shiner hung beneath his left eye. He swung out each leg and sat on the edge of the bed, his wrought skin the color of rained-on sand. Head bent low, he lit a cigarette and hacked. Watching the smoke he thought how, like a scorned lover, the body reacts poorly to neglect. In the sheets behind him, a mess of blonde hair stirred across a smooth shoulder stitched with skulls and sparrow wings, a trail of ink continuing down her naked body. He followed the tattoo back to the part of her face visible between hair and the pillow. Nothing reminded him of her name.

In fact, not much came back after last night's set at Bourbon & Boots, one of the most worn-out shitholes in all of San Antonio. Some prick had to go and point out how Jordan played guitar like his father. "I mean exactly, no two ways about it. You two is kindred, I tell you what," the man had slurred. There was little that lit his blood more than that. It was true, of course, he just hated hearing it. If anybody cared to compare, Jordan's presence on stage was a depressing spectacle when matched against the polish of his old man.

His first chords rang from a Twin Reverb over the din of the drunks, then Jordan closed his eyes and leaned into the microphone. His occasionally accurate tenor came out like he had gravel in his throat. After two he broke, sipped a well drink, rolled his checkered sleeves, then got back stomping that hollow wood, wailing about gut-sick hours lost in some highway motel. A few couples danced beneath the lone light, and he wondered again why that asshole had to crack about his pa.

He could Travis-pick his way out of a toilet stall faster than his father ever could. He could run those jaunty little Piedmont rags even if they were too lighthearted for a man of his ragged sensibilities. He could do it, though, which was the point. When he played on the couch at home on hot Texas nights, he fell in love with the brutal wind that blew from his chrome National. When he lingered too hard on fourths and minor sevens, bile kicked up the back of his tongue. Those diminished runs more often than not took an evening and drowned it in the river out of mercy. A far cry from the name in lights he always associated with his father. Jordan had been disappearing from the headline his whole life. Walker Bayne, "Mr. Bluegrass" from the Ozarks to Nashville and both coasts to Europe. He sang alongside country's last heroes and sped across the South pitching perfect harmonies and garbling banjo rolls so fast they only translated on speed and corn whiskey in places they're far from messing around about anything. So yes, he got his picking from that unreliable miser. His tune, too. Every Goddamned thing. But Jordan would never play one of his songs.

The crowd had filled in and a smiling woman hoisted a drink through the dark. Jordan reached down and grabbed it before she disappeared back into the amorphous heap. Crowds and drunks bothered him on the rare night, like one in Phoenix four years ago, when a guy tried to make off with the entire microphone stand while it was still plugged in. Jordan caught him by the shirt and swung him around, arms out straight like a nervous prom date, kicked him once in the gut, doubling him over, then without thinking busted his nose, sending a thin film of blood across the stage. He recalled the silence that followed the fat man's body crashing through the speakers. He had a good laugh about it later as he attempted to get comfortable for the night in his jail cell.

Jordan wrapped up the set, laid his guitar in its case backstage, and walked back out front. The burly tender put up whiskey and water. Jordan emptied the drink and the bartender filled it again. Jordan hit it and exhaled. Sweat stuck brown tendrils of hair down the sides of his seamless scruff. His mind was empty and calm after performing. He slouched on planted elbows, the fist in his gut loosened, and in no time at all a good-looking woman was drawing out his bone-white laugh.

Mae was half-Mexican and half-clothed. She kissed Jordan's cheek and hung her warm hand around the back of his neck. "Awpahh," she said, wiping her mouth. "You're wetter than a dog." She handed Jordan a shot, winked, then tipped hers to the ceiling. "Sunrises go down easy 'cause I ain't got no gag reflex."

Jordan cocked an eye at her. "I don't want to know nothin' about that."

"Sure you do," she said. Her breath climbed up the knots in his neck. She asked if he was all right.

They always ask that, he thought, trading a new sigh into a cold beer.

A drunk named Skunk stared at Mae in the mirror behind the rack of bottles, his rotten-toothed mouth frozen with arousal, his odor impossible to ignore. It wasn't street-level rank, just a lifetime spent being poor and soused. He edged an emaciated ass cheek onto an open stool and out of something like empathy Jordan ordered them both beers and Skunk the extra shot. He only had to suffer the unconvincing smile of the drunk, his eyes trained on keeping the liquid inside the rim of each glass as he shuffled away

Jordan got up and talked at a table with Marcos and Hernando, two stocky Salvadorans burnt the color of ink from twelve-hour days in a pepper field. He liked them because they were both good-humored and kind, and also because he had that job once, for less than a month eight or nine years ago, until one morning he went to pick up water and cigarettes and just kept driving.

The three of them stepped outside to smoke. The humidity of late day had been tamed by night, and there was the blonde from his bed, lighting a cigarette by her car in low-cut boots, high shorts, and a ripped shirt slid off of one shoulder. They got to talking. After a time, not long, her lips were parted by a sultry whisper. "How much longer you staying tonight?"

He stood from the bed, lit a Camel, and checked his cell. Just after noon and one message. Blue smoke trailed as he sat at the kitchen table and closed his eyes while the message played.

"Ah just said I am. It's ringin' now," a belligerent woman droned. "I's only calling to wish the scumbag son of Newton County a sad and miserable evening. See, we all heard rumor your sorry no-good motherfuckin' ass was gon' be back here for your brother's wedding."

Other voices contributed to the cacophony. "Better ain't catch you back ere, faggit!"

"Ah told you," she explained to the ape at her side. "Brianna's brother, who owns the Grocery Lot on 413—yeah, that one— they got insurance from that place Malcolm worked all them years. Any fuckin' way, a group ah us was just here thinking back on what a useless piece of shit y'ar."

Disconcerting, how laughter grows heinous in groups.

"Thar's a table here, hell thar's a whole bar a people that would just love to tell it to your face, but you ain't been round here in years. An ah guess we're all just real used to that. Get what I'm saying?"

Growls and hollers and swipes for the phone. "Hey, tell that motherfucker," a man began, drowned out by a loud scream. The woman's voice distorted and Jordan wondered whether or not he knew her. He found it prescient how she cupped her hand around the receiver to make sure she was heard.

"Ah'll tell 'im, ah said ah'm telling 'im. If ah were you, ah'dn't be showing your face. There's plenty more trouble than you could ever cause back here waitin'."

The early morning sun had been beating the apartment for hours. Thin walls, cheap leather couch, yellowed blinds tinged with dust, table covered in garbage and ash, the bed and the girl all held the heat like a lung of wet smoke. Jordan pulled on jeans and a white T-shirt and opened the front door, pouring a river of fresh air along the tile floor up across the blonde's porcelain body. She raised an eye as Jordan stuffed clothes from his dresser into a bag. The glass in the fridge door clinked. He leaned in head first and emerged with half a wrapped sandwich, a plastic container of strawberries, orange juice, and four bottles of Presidente.

He bent over the bed and kissed her. She held his arm, running her hands over his broad shoulders and through his hair, crossing the mess of tissue that filled one side of his face with dried blood.

"Oh, baby," she said. "How's the eye?" She put her lips on the contour of his bruise.

"I've narrowed it down to a person or the floor that did it, not sure which one."

He tied his boots, then piled the bag of food, clothes, and his guitar case in the passenger seat of his truck. The screen door clapped again on his way back in as he searched the table for his sunglasses. A big pile of keys sang in his palm while he straight-

ened a pile of mail, turned off a lamp, and ran his hand down the
wall to turn off a power switch.

"Where you off to?" she called from the bed.

"Let yourself out whenever you like. Don't rush on account
of me or anything."

"You're leaving me here?" She sat up, confused. "Well, what
if I decide to stay?"

"I don't care what you do. You might have a week or two before the property manager comes around. He's all right. His name
is Juan. He plays chess." Jordan stretched his back, doing his best
to work out the pain still needling through his side. Behind his
sunglasses, he paused to take in another beautiful girl he knew he
would never see again. "I'm going home."

TWO

IT WAS ODD TO say, but Malcolm Bayne had a talent for insurance. He got his start at seventeen when he begged for a job as a file clerk at a company called Ringgold a half hour from his house and had practiced nothing but that approximate science ever since. The way the industry calculated risk by breaking the world into categories like fault, force, and blame made a perverse amount of sense to him. Malcolm learned everything he could about his clients—income and debt, probate and penury, genetic predisposition and psychopathology—until he revealed the abhorrent truth behind each façade.

Malcolm learned to trust his understanding of the almost imperceptible difference between calculated and unforeseen risks. An entire world of threats could be grouped together in a few predictable ways. Most were bound by some degree of commonality, only the rare case proved traumatic or inhumane. House fires, highway accidents, encephalitis. Rich housewives who gambled with matches, widowed spouses who'd lost the will to live. Each act exhibited a pattern. Even acts of God. What appeared to the world as a complex problem was revealed to Malcolm as a simple truth that could be dealt with, or at least easily mitigated. Every small victory over disorder brought its own satisfaction. The joy Malcolm found in his work come from that assurance. Not the presence of something positive, just the absence of fear.

Thin and darkly serious, Malcolm pulled on the fat misplaced at the bottom of his cheeks. He stood with his back to the empty conference table, studying the liquid curve of his reflection in a wall of windows. The ninth floor of the Garnet building looked out on everything in Little Rock east of MacArthur Park to the river. An impress of clouds textured the sunlit glass in which Malcolm saw his boss charge in behind him, clapping enthusiastically.

"What fresh hell you come from, boy?" His boss hugged him with desperate rigor as he snapped out of his contemplation. He motioned for Malcolm to follow him back to his office, where they stood in front of his desk and sipped coffee.

"Your work on primary accounts really put us ahead this summer. Well-deserved time off, well-deserved. Too bad you have to spend it getting married."

Malcolm let his boss's eruption of laughter at his own joke subside.

"Where's the ceremony again?"

"Back home," Malcolm told him. "Newton County. The house where I grew up, actually."

"Don't tell me you're up there on the Buffalo River."

"Not on the Buffalo, but it's nearby," said Malcolm.

The boss pointed at Malcolm's chest, swashing his coffee. "See, that's smart. Janie and me had our wedding here in town. Small fortune, of course. Today? This economy?" He squinted at the ceiling and stopped talking as though he had unexpectedly come face to face with another, far graver notion. Then he asked how beautiful the country was out there.

"It's not the sort of place you go back that often. It's not a place people leave, either. My family's been on that land since the Civil War. Supposedly, it's in our blood."

His boss stretched, exposing a triangle of heaving stomach under his striped shirt. "Hell, that long, it is your blood. The Bayne clan, couple of true Arkies."

Malcolm attended one last meeting under diffuse halogen. He hurried back to his desk, powered down his computer, and wrangled loose papers into the fold of his leather bag. Lou, who worked across from him, avoided making eye contact through the open door. A miniature basketball hoop hung from the upholstered wall of his cubicle beside the football schedule of his alma mater. Malcolm stood at the corner of the partition, pressing down the plastic net and watching it spring back up again. "Hey, Lou," he said in a hushed tone, "have fun watching the Razorbacks lose this weekend."

Lou swung his pleated legs from under his chair, politely asked an elderly woman to hold on the phone, covered his black goatee and the receiver and said, "Have fun getting married, pussy."

From an early age, Malcolm was at his best when he succeeded in beating back abstractions from his mind. When he and his twin brother Jordan were kids, they traded in skills and traits the other possessed—hunting for scouting, math for music, athletics for book smarts, logic for brute force. Jordan not only taught Malcolm how to fight, he even taught him how to play. Not how games were supposed to go, necessarily, but how to relax enough to let himself make believe. In turn, Malcolm urged him to avoid confrontations and stay out of trouble.

The effort didn't take, to say the least.

By the time they were teenagers, they barely spoke. Jordan was beyond reproach and Malcolm was already wrenching free from the hills that raised him. Though obsession with constant progress was the engine that drove him, lately a storm of loud,

pointless thoughts had seeped in and showed no signs of relent-
ing. He blamed it on the stress of the wedding and perhaps, too,
the prospect of returning home—though he would never admit it.

His new townhouse stood lit on the edge of night. Malcolm
parked and slouched in the driver's seat long enough for the
driveway motion light to switch back off. He loosened his tie and
watched his fiancé Elizabeth framed in warm light in the window
one story up, her face tapered like a hawk's breast. Steam rose
from the sink, condensing on the windowpane as she caressed a
bowl beneath a steady stream of water.

When he lumbered through the door, Elizabeth pulled herself up on his collar and kissed him. "How punctual," she said.
"Dinner is served." As they ate, they discussed their last-minute
wedding checklist, finishing a bottle of red in the process. After
two hours of television, Malcolm fell asleep on the couch and
was roused awake by the graze of Elizabeth's hair. He leaned
up to meet her gentle kiss. He held one of her tanned thighs
and kept his balance on the edge of the cushion as he drove his
weight between her legs. After, they put the couch back together
and straightened the rest of the house. Elizabeth lazily switched
off the lights and dragged herself to bed, curling in a ball against
Malcolm's back.

The next morning they headed north through city and west
through suburbs before the road turned languorous through farms
and trees and wound its way into the heart of the hills.

STEAK $10, PRAISE JESUS. Jordan's truck was caked with two hundred
miles of north Texas dirt when he pulled off the windblown shoulder and came to a stop in front of a little diner, windows scored
with sand, paint faded and cracked by the sun. A bell screwed to
the heel of the door rang as Jordan pushed it open. A wiry trucker

leered from under his cowboy hat, sipped a beaded can of Coke
and looked away. Young hips swayed to the edge of the table.

"Something to aid your constitution?" she asked.

Jordan ordered one of those steaks from the sign, then stared
out past the cars across a desolate plane howled by dust. The sun
broke land and sky into refractions of gold, honeysuckle, and a
funereal scarlet that thinned on the far reach of the horizon. He
hadn't been back through the Ouachita highlands for over twenty
years, when he would camp every summer with his friend Russ
and his family. Jordan hated when his brother came along because
Malcolm would always catch more fish than him. Malcolm tried to
hand Jordan his line when a fish was on, but he could not stand
being patronized so he would disappear into the woods for hours,
shooting squirrels with a BB gun, using his folding knife to whittle
a branch to a point and then stab it through the tiny carcasses.
Then the boys would drag their rods, tackle, and a bucket of dead
fish and squirrel meat through high brush and rough terrain back
to the campsite.

After all these years, Jordan remained mystified by his brother.
His intelligence, his preternatural awareness. He had to listen close
if he hoped to decode Malcolm's peculiar way of speaking. For
instance, in their tent out there under the stars, Malcolm used to
look up and say how the days were signatures, each with its own
feel, texture, and shape. Every unique form dictated what was able
to occur in that space at that time. Each day becoming aware of
itself as it determined its purpose and unfolded its own fate. Signatures, Jordan thought as he stared out the window. He never
knew what that meant, and to think of it now, he still didn't. Malcolm used to say the universe was in flux. Once you thought you
understood one aspect of something, if you happened to come
upon it another way, you would find a new ordering of an entirely

other reality there. He could never understand how his brother thought so succinctly about such abstract things. For Jordan, those thoughts invited doubt and unrealized outcomes that only intimidated him. He imagined seeing his brother again and wondered what the ordering of his new reality might look like.

The waitress handed over a steak and a beer, then asked where Jordan was coming from.

"San Antonio," he said. The dispassion in his voice echoed back to him.

"I was thinking of moving to Arlington with my friend," the waitress said brightly. "They got this nursing program there, you know, down by Forth Worth?"

He washed the air with his hand. "I'm from Arkansas, originally."

"That where you headed to?"

"Excuse me?" He squinted up at her. Sometimes his hearing went out.

"What are you heading back to?"

"I couldn't possibly say."

He thanked her for the food, sipped his beer, and ate in quiet.

Twenty minutes later he dropped a smoldering butt to the gravel then climbed back in his truck and got up to speed on the blacktop. Far back in the lot, beside a dumpster and low-hanging tree, a '59 Fleetwood gurgled in park. Two men sat on the white leather bench seat, obscured from view. A tall old man with a black mountain dasher had a long gray beard that blew across the newspaper he had folded open on the wheel. Beside him sat a short gentleman with parted hair and a tan suit, scribbling in a heavily notated binder. The older one kept his eyes on the direction in which Jordan just sped, hot air blowing off the highway.

"It appears as though he is on course." The little man spoke without raising his head. "He should be headed east on 62 and cross the state line near Prairie Grove."

"He'll be at the house by nightfall," the tall one said with certainty. His withered voice was softer than parchment. The Fleetwood slid into drive and pulled onto the road, far enough behind Jordan not to be seen.

THREE

THE FOYER OF THE Bayne house was decorated with family heirlooms and old photographs. Two inseparable infants on their backs in a pen. Dusty-haired boys with proud smiles flanking their father in front of a gleaming Eldorado. Shirtless, skinny adolescents abreast the portside of a Crestliner, squinting onto the verdigris rush of the White River. Jordan traced his callused fingers along ruby vines coiled beneath fat cherubim on a French vase before being startled by his own wild hair and dirty reflection in the mirror above the mantle, which were both heirlooms of his great-grandmother, Eleanora.

He leaned over the bottom of the stairwell and looked up at the shadowed landing on the second floor. Someone turned on a faucet upstairs, so he rushed over to the living room and stood at the curtains, hoping not to be seen. He looked onto the gravel drive and the barn, the sole remaining features of the original property. The eight-by-eight trusses, elm floors, and pine clapboard had been cut and planed by hand from the surrounding trees. The rest of the cropper house burned in 1886, a fire that also claimed two lives.

Bayne land came up from the road a good fifty acres, lush with third growth and untamed brush. When they were kids, Malcolm and Jordan made a game of navigating the briar in the far back of the yard. They discovered a rare opening where the thicket grew thin enough for them to twist their young bodies through the thorns. The first time they broke through they braved the brush on their bellies, covered in dirt and sorrel, leaving cuts on arms and raspberry abrasions on elbows and knees. They brushed off and straightened jeans tucked into boots, drew sweatshirt hoods tight, and ran free as their flashlights bounced across their new domain.

They walked for a while before Malcolm noticed the iridescent sky widen overhead as they approached the clearing. Twisted weald and chaparral spread toward a huge flowering elm tree that sulked over the bank of a small pond. At first they were convinced a grove that magical could only exist in their imaginations. They ran and jumped across the overgrown earth and eventually came to stand beneath the canopy of the elm. Malcolm foraged around for the perfect stone and pulled one from the ground. Jordan watched his brother approach the edge of the water and drop the rock, rippling the black surface to its farthest edge. It was then that they knew this place they had discovered was in fact real, and that it would be their first secret.

In the kitchen, Jordan fished a cold bottle out of the refrigerator and heard voices from the backyard. He stepped onto the back deck to find Malcolm and his father talking on the lawn in twilight.

"A ghost walks before us," Walker called out.

Jordan united them both with a hug. Malcolm grabbed his brother and landed a slap on his back. "My brother, in the flesh."

Walker had no regard for predictions, but he wasn't sure Jordan would show. That didn't matter now. He couldn't help but acknowledge the ardent love he held for his son. They studied each other, their light-tinged eyes sparkling with relief.

"All right, let's get it out of the way. I missed you," Jordan con-
fessed to his brother. "Just kidding, I didn't really miss you. That's
just something people say." He looked around. "Hey, where's Elizabeth? You are marrying the girl, figure I should meet her."

Malcolm landed a shot in his ribs. "She was upstairs, she'll
be—well, never mind."

"If this ain't the cutest thing I ever saw," Elizabeth exclaimed
from the deck.

Jordan traced the sweet Carolina drawl to a round, cheery face
bronzed by porch light, framed by thin strands of hair that fell
behind Elizabeth's ears and down her slender shoulders.

"Meet my bride, Elizabeth May Truitt," said Malcolm.

"How in the world did you trick a girl like that into marrying
you?" Jordan whispered.

"Easy," said Malcolm. "She hadn't met any of y'all until tonight."

Elizabeth dispensed a round of beers then handed hers to
Malcolm and bounced into Jordan's arms, planting the most pla-
tonic kiss Jordan's cheek had ever felt. She compared Jordan to the
image she had of him in her mind. Most of what she had heard
was hyperbole, the stuff of legend. Now, face to face, she found
him to be kind, scrappy, and sort of aloof, his posture reminding
her of a kicked dog.

Swinging his beer bottle like a processional bell, Jordan
called for a toast. "May the best day of your past be the worst
day of your future." He considered what he had just said. "I
think that's how it goes. Anyway, to a wonderful wedding," he
proclaimed.

Elizabeth washed the strain of awe from her throat with a
swill of beer and continued the oratory tone. "To y'all being together again, and to our families being joined together from this
point on. To what joy may come," she said sweetly.

The Baynes had been pried apart by time, scattered across the ages. The very concept of family lay with other monoliths of love and trust partly submerged in some strange, forgetful tide. What a notion, Jordan thought, that it could go the other way, too.

On the dinner table sat plates heaped with roasted chicken, carrots, and cornbread. Elizabeth told Walker the smell reminded her of home.

"As far as cooking for myself goes, I have three recipes down. This is one of them," he told her. "The other two come out of a can."

"We're very grateful," she said, looking around the table.

"Yeah, thanks, Pa," Malcolm added.

"We had these big summer meals in our backyard. Ours was North Carolina barbecue, of course, just a touch sweeter," Elizabeth continued. "Most of the vegetables were from my aunt Ashley's garden. She had these fruit trees that would ripen that time of year, too. Apples, peaches, blackberries, you name it. My mom, my aunt, and I would walk the grass barefoot, our buckets overflowing with fruit. After dinner we would gather on the porch and wait for night to set. The air was so thick you could swim through the sky." Elizabeth held a buttered square of cornbread in front of her, studying it. "My other aunt, Margaret, her cornbread was just heaven. This sure gives it a run for its money, though." She smiled then devoured half the yellow bread.

"Are they coming to the wedding?" Jordan asked.

She sipped her water. "That's right. My momma, Mary, Aunts Margaret and Ashley, their husbands Alan and Mike, and all their kids."

Jordan asked if they were all back in North Carolina.

She nodded. "Momma still lives in the house I grew up in on the Outer Banks. Aunt Ashley's family is just outside Wilmington. The rest are coming in from Chicago."

"How about the boys, Jordan? They coming to the wedding?" Malcolm asked.

"Haven't kept in touch with most folks round here. I should be asking you, it's your wedding," said Jordan.

"They were your friends."

"Who, you mean Harrell?" Jordan asked.

"Harrell, Baron, that prick Russ. Those knuckleheads better not show up just to wreak havoc on our special day."

"We'll see, won't we?" Jordan teased.

Elizabeth snorted the condensation of a laugh into her glass, then dripped the last red drops in a line on her tongue. She reached out the bottle to refill Walker's wine glass, but he raised his hand after the first splash.

"Not drinking, Pa?" Jordan asked.

"Not supposed to with these pills they got me on. A small amount will do. Speaking of," he patted the pocket of his flannel, "I am supposed to take them with food. I'll be right back."

"Nonsense, let me get them for you." Elizabeth helped herself up and Walker told her where to find the leather bag in his bathroom.

"So, how's life for an old man in the country? Rubin, Ross, and them still around?" Malcolm asked.

Walker grumbled and stroked the scruff around his mouth. "We fish an arm of the Buffalo once a week and play cards Wednesday nights when Rubin's wife volunteers at the big church where that gay pastor resigned."

Elizabeth returned with the bag. "Your carvings," she said. "I saw the ducks on the mantle and the bench downstairs. I meant to ask you earlier."

"That's just something to pass the quiet," he said. "Don't have to worry about that no more. This wedding's got things all stirred up around here."

Elizabeth stood behind Walker's chair and rubbed his shoulders. "Oh, it won't be so bad," she promised.

"Not if you keep that up," he said, patting her wrist. "You're beautiful, the two of you. Proud of this boy here." Walker rested his heavy eyes on Malcolm, who stirred and looked away.

He switched his tone to Jordan. "Been playin'?"

Jordan slouched under his hat, fortifying himself against the question.

Walker unzipped the small leather bag and pulled out a multitude of bottles.

"Damn, they got you on the whole pharmacy," Malcolm said.

Walker sorted the bottles on the edge of the table. "Let's see," he said, blowing the air from his cheeks. "Quinapril's for my blood pressure, Seroquel for insomnia, I take Xarelto and these horsepill ibuprofens 'cause of my leg, oh and beta blockers for a heart thing." He peered blindly at the bottle. "What's this one? That's not even a real word. They can't just make up words like that."

"Heart thing?" Jordan interjected. "You mean a heart attack?"

"It wasn't as bad as all that. Doctor said it was minor."

"That's still a heart attack! Why didn't you tell us?" He looked at his brother. "Did you know?"

"How would I know? You could've died," Malcolm said, turning to his father.

"Then you two would have had to get along for once, figure out what to do with me."

The boys exchanged wounded glances. Elizabeth sank in the pressure of mediation. "They are here now and they are concerned about you, Walker. This whole thing is just going to take some," she paused to choose the correct word, "time."

"This family, I swear," Jordan muttered, shaking his head.

"What's that?" Walker sat up, stern with anger. "What was I supposed to say to you, boy? I don't even know how to reach you half the time. I bet your brother you weren't even going to show up here tonight."

"You have my number," Jordan said.

"Which one is that? I ain't seen you in so long. You think I'm just going to call if I need something, or to let you know how I'm *feeling*?" Walker let out a terse laugh. "If I held out for you I'd be deader than dirt."

Rage wavered in the corners of Jordan's eyes like black flags in the wind. "I ain't been home in some time, true, but it ain't like you ever came calling on me to see how I was." He pointed across the table. "Did you get down to Little Rock to see Elizabeth and him? It's only a three, four-hour drive. You could have spent the night."

"That's rich coming from you," said Walker. "From what I understand, you never stopped by neither. I remember, Malcolm told me you even played a show out there when your brother was in college and you just drove on through. Must've been real busy."

"I had my own problems to deal with and I did, with no help from either of you."

"Fuck you," Malcolm spit.

"Fuck all of you." Jordan roared to his feet then paused for a second. "Not you," he said to Elizabeth and lumbered from the table.

"Guess we're not having pie." Malcolm slid his chair back to get up.

"Sit your ass down," Elizabeth said in a huff. She whipped herself up and deposited the dirtied plates in the kitchen, trading them for clean bowls and spoons. Walker and Malcolm sat brooding until Elizabeth placed a bowl in front of each of them and dropped the pie with a thud on the center of the table. "Eat," she commanded.

"Well," said Walker. "Suppose I'll get the brandy."

FOUR

DAWN SEEPED THROUGH THE HILLS. Walker stood in the early morning light, waiting for the kettle to cough steam. After a life spent singing and picking, he found solitude and prolonged quiet the most musical of all. There was only one problem, as much as he hated to admit. A tremendous boredom overtook him if he was awake for too many hours in a day. He often rose hours before first light. Household chores, busywork, and numerous hobbies were not enough of a distraction. Nights he did not play cards, he read passages from the Bible he had already pored over countless times. Even still, Walker heeded Peter, that one day with the Lord was a thousand years and a thousand years one day. If he still found himself awake, there was always tobacco to smoke and wood to carve.

Walker halted the hiss of steam and poured the boiling water over grounds heaped in a filter. With the boys back in the house he was temporarily relieved, if not of the ravages of old age, over which he knew he had no control, then at least of the loneliness that always knew to attack when he was at his weakest, forcing an end to long stretches where he was perfectly content being alone. As if out of nowhere, in the simplest, most routine moments, he would go through a sort of awakening while he was still awake and would come to the realization that he was trapped—in his head, in that hour, his whole life. Stripped of his defenses, Walker could do nothing but watch as his options of where to go or what to do or who to do it with fell helplessly away. All that remained for him was to merely exist. To suffer the burn of a present where time never commenced and nothing was ever altered.

Walker sipped his coffee and witnessed the mists lift off the backyard. He had developed an eye for the birds in the surrounding woods and knew what time of year and even what hour of day they often arrived. What was lost to a person who did not know what to look for was registered by Walker in the blink of an eye. Two kestrels, dotted black and ember, emerged with the sun and landed in the dewy grass with a prolonged thrush of wings. Juncos, kites, and kinglets streaked through azure flows of sky. A pair of warblers, pocked olive and pollen, sifted from cover in stands of pine behind the barn. A copse of pine that grew so thick with underbrush that Walker had to hack it back by hand each spring.

The aroma of coffee stirred Jordan on the couch. He sat up shirtless and coughed for a good minute while Walker fixed a mug with aqueous black and handed it to his son. Jordan yawned and took the cup. "Thanks," he said, squinting against the bright wall of windows. "Can't remember the last time I woke up here."

"You're telling me," said Walker. "I had to pour a whole other cup of coffee."

Walker spread his gaze around at the walls and furniture, realizing he never so much as passed through the living room when no one else was in the house. "You're up now," he said and slapped Jordan's bare shoulder. Walker folded back one of the curtains and flooded the room with daylight.

Gentle footsteps came up from behind. Elizabeth kissed Walker and Jordan each on the cheek and announced that breakfast would soon be served. Jordan was still trying to get the front half of his brain working. He gulped his coffee, confounded by the blonde hair and smooth legs that bounced down the hall toward the kitchen. Elizabeth pulled flour from the pantry and butter, syrup, and fresh berries from the fridge.

"Nice having a woman fix breakfast," Walker said.

Malcolm joined his father and brother in the living room and Elizabeth handed him a cup of coffee. He sat beside Jordan on the couch then cleared a space among bottles, keys, and cigarettes to set his cup.

"If you insist on staying down here, you should at least straighten up."

Jordan stayed quiet, hovered over his coffee. Malcolm shrugged it off and asked him what he had going on for the day.

"I'm in meetings all morning," Jordan said, amused. "We could go out tonight. You know, if you're around." He wrangled his jeans from the floor and buckled them on.

Elizabeth yelled from the kitchen. "Hon, we've got to leave soon to pick up Ma and Aunt Mary, they arrive at 12:48 in Fayetteville. I don't want to be late."

Malcolm held a sip in his mouth and pushed his cheeks out like a full bladder, suppressing whatever he was going to say. Jordan gathered from his silence that Malcolm was contractually obligated to retrieve his in-laws from the airport.

Malcolm raised his voice to reach Elizabeth over the frying of the griddle. "The car does have GPS, you know."

"Don't even," she warned, flipping a pancake.

Malcolm and Elizabeth left to retrieve her family and Jordan found himself alone in the house with his father. They meandered together at a slow pace down the hall that led to Walker's music room. Gilded plaques, awards, and pictures lined the walls, testaments to Walker's time in the trenches of American music. Gaunt and uncaring in a Stetson, donning a gray double-breasted suit onstage with an old Liberty. Smoking on the street outside the RCA building in Nashville, posing alongside Lee Hays, Don Everly, and blind Leon Payne. Jordan asked his father about a photograph where he was wearing headphones and sticking out his tongue in a wood-paneled studio booth.

"My bassist, Jim Cleary, was giving me the finger on the other side of the glass while we were tracking vocals on 'Late, Great, and Second Rate.'" He leaned in, studying the frame. "We were staying at our manager's girlfriend's apartment in south Kansas City, a block from the studio. Those were what they call the good old days with Rubin, Jimmy, and Greg. Lacy Duvall sat in on that record. She was on the tour, too. We did the album and then toured for eighteen months straight. A different stage in a different city every night. We had so much momentum, we couldn't be stopped. That was our best record," he said. "We played like hell on that thing." He pointed at another photograph high up on the wall. "This one here was the same tour, but at the end. We headed west to San Francisco, then instead of playing our way back we flew out and did Boston, Philadelphia, then Carnegie Hall in New York. I remember the way it sounded, just pure. I remember I could follow what I was playing as it rifled around the hall, and at the same time I could hear the snap of someone's fingers or sit there and have a regular conversation with the guy on the other side of the stage. It was unlike anything I ever heard."

Jordan harbored a number of very specific grudges against his father over the years. Some he was aware of, others not. One of them was his success as a musician. The petty simplicity of that hatred now embarrassed him as he stood there, quietly listening.

"I never wanted to leave New York," Walker continued. "I must have stayed three weeks out on Long Island, and back in the city I stayed in Harlem. The country scene and jazz scene had these giants, but it was rare when they overlapped. So one night, in a packed apartment on 128th Street, I ended up meeting Bud Powell. He had this larger-than-life reputation, you know. Boy, could he drink. Ended up killing him. There was a piano in the parlor and he got on with a trumpet player. I didn't know how you could play so loud in a building with other tenants like that. It didn't make any sense, but they were stars of the neighborhood. I guess everybody enjoyed it so much nobody complained."

Jordan followed Walker into the music room. Soundproof panels hung between support beams, sound-absorbing carpet sealed the floor. The air was hot and dry to keep the instruments in ideal condition. The room had not changed in over thirty years. Walker's acoustic and electric guitars, banjos, mandolins, fiddles, Dobros, a pedal steel, and several handmade dulcimers adorned the racks that spread evenly across the walls. The atmosphere was calm and resolute in its devotion to harmony, rhythm, and soul, the creation of music being one of the few forms of piety to which the Baynes ever adhered.

A river of cords snaked up to amplifiers and speakers. Walker told Jordan to pick up a guitar while he worked his heavy body onto a stool and sat a steel Dobro in his lap. Walker fidgeted as he pushed the bottleneck on his ring finger. "My fingers are too fat for the slide," he said. "Lord help me."

Jordan held a saddle-hipped Martin 17 and nested his palm in the crevice worn into the wood. The guitar had been played for so many years that the finish had faded and revealed the smooth, textured grain of the body, like driftwood on a beach. Walker slid a lick that rang from the metal. Jordan came in behind him, nervous,

He paid attention to the casual changes of blues in E and followed his father as he would in a conversation. Walker nodded for Jordan to take it for a walk so he broke into a full galloping roll, pulling off thirds and pinching sevenths before winding back to the beginning, when Walker took over again with a high-pitched metallic wave from his Dobro. Jordan admired the way his father picked with the ease and effortless control of someone who had played that instrument their entire lives. They had never once played guitars together.

Walker hung the Dobro back in its place on the wall, then threw on his jacket and zipped it over his chest. "I have to head into town to run some errands," he said. "Propane for the wedding, some groceries. I'll be back tonight for the barbecue." Walker patted Jordan's neck, his hand hard and warm. "That was fun, we'll do it again sometime." Jordan watched his father's lugubrious shape skulk into the garage.

Alone in the quiet, Jordan sat with the instruments. Emblems of a life that ran congruous to his but had remained inaccessible until now. He got up and flipped the switch on a record player. He pulled a beer from the mini fridge and perused the disarray of papers and opened mail strewn about Walker's desk. A letter requesting Walker's attendance at an event, a royalty statement, a bill for remodeling the kitchen, a gun catalog. A deck of cards sat on a round table. He pictured Walker playing cards with his friends, listening to records, drinking alone. He sauntered over to a bookshelf behind the desk, where a row of leather-bound photo albums caught his eye.

Jordan pulled one of the albums and kicked his feet up at the desk as he flipped through the plastic-sleeved pages. The photos were from a period similar to those in the hall, but these were all personal. He spread the book open to a three-by-three of Walker posing in front of an Eldorado with his brother, Jacob. Jordan had not seen or heard mention of his uncle for so long it took a moment to recognize him. Jordan didn't know if he was still alive. There were more pictures with faded corners, of summers on the porch, fixing cars, fishing. He flipped back to the previous page. Jacob and Walker shielded their eyes from the sun with the same posture, squinting, heads tilted, right hands curved over their brows like a salute. They stood casually by Walker's old car in the same relaxed stance. Every essence was similar. Not identical, just repeated.

The hair on the back of his neck stood on end. "They're *twins?*" he muttered aloud. Confounded, he placed the album back on the shelf with the others and listened as the last song on the record played out.

FIVE

1976—THE BEAR ATTACK

Walker came home weary from two months of shows. It wasn't raining, but it should have been. The RTS streamliner glided past a desolate park on the riverfront and coughed into the Little Rock depot. A cadre of hungover, homesick bandmates who had spent every waking moment together for the past sixty days departed the bus without a word and found their own lone roads back, hoping home was still the way they had left it.

Wind tumbled under electric clouds that followed Walker out of the city. He rolled down the window of his brown Eldorado and the pressure of the air bore through the pinprick in his damaged ear, sending a high-pitched siren straight to his brain. He drove the winding roads squinting one eye shut and struggling to keep the wheel straight until he pulled into his driveway. Debris blew across the lawn When he came in through the downstairs, the house radiated a stillness made all the more fragile by the anticipation of it being ruined. The walls in the corridor tilted and wavered. A sick feeling rose from his waist. Walker teetered on the bottom stair, suitcase and bag in hand, worried by what awaited him. He peeked into the nursery at Malcolm and Jordan before he went to the bedroom, where his wife Mercy stood by the far side of their bed.

"Leave 'em packed," she said, eyeing his bags. Her black hair flowed around the knit of a charcoal shawl, voice worn from anger slowly turning into sorrow. Neither possessed the energy to plead, whether it was Mercy demanding repentance or Walker begging for forgiveness. He knew why she was upset. He could not convince her of what he had not done—change. To fight would only further insult her, so he kept his mouth shut. She suspected he had a girl in Atlanta, and she was right. They had played two shows through Georgia and Walker hadn't called home for the better part of that week. What Mercy did not know was how the girl rode with them all the way to D.C., how they spent their time together getting high and lying strikingly still, not speaking or moving. She was backstage, in the bus, rarely left his side. It was one of those things Walker could never say, because to say it was to be condemned.

Mercy knew Walker's father Maurel was planning to bring him and Jacob on their annual hunting trip. The time away would give Mercy space to think, and she told Walker he should use the time to decide where he would go upon his return. They looked at each other, so far apart, farther than the dimensions of the room could have allowed.

"I love you, Mercy. You have to know that." He fought his indefensible position as she turned away and cried. He looked down in shame, both bags still clutched in his hands. He hadn't even set them down.

The barrel of his hunting rifle stuck through the trees. Walker waited until the deer was so close he could see her hair twitch. The fawn searched around before lowering her nose in the grass. That was when Walker fired. The missed shot sent the skinny fawn bounding from sight. Jacob and Maurel poked fun at Walker for missing at close range. An hour later, Jacob hit a two-point buck from over a hundred and fifty yards through cover. "Don't worry," Jacob taunted his brother. "I'll let you dress it."

Sheets of meat separated from knotted cartilage and rigid clefts of bone. Walker struggled through slippery viscous to make even cuts in the sinew. He got out the best meat first, from the hindquarter to loins, stabbing into the body with a quiet jealously that he hid from Jacob and his father as they reclined on a felled log, smoking. He skinned the fine-haired pelt with precision, removed the last of the vitals, and tossed the sack in the dirt for the coyotes. He went down to the water and washed his bloody arms in a nearby creek.

Walker moped around the campsite, worried sick about losing Mercy forever. He did not say a word through dinner. Sloughing off his camp chair, he sat in the dirt, sipping off a bottle and staring into the fire. Maurel took a seat behind him, patted his shoulder and told him, in a matter-of-fact way, to do everything possible in order to save the marriage.

"If you are stubborn, let it go," Maurel said. "Whatever it is, it's doomed, anyhow. Chances are virtue ain't on your side, so tell her she's right. Even if she ain't, tell her a thousand times. Ain't nothing worth defending in this life. You'll end up with all that pride, alone. If it's your ways you're worried about, change every last one of them. They're not worth shit in the end."

Walker kept his eye on the folding flames. Maurel pulled off the bottle and handed it back to his son, his expression dropping to the depths of his own painful past. "I never did that with your mother," he said. "I could have talked more, only I never knew what to say. Still, I should have stayed and worked through it with her, would have been fairer to you and your brother. Instead, I left her at the first sign of struggle. Had to learn each lesson the hard way, I guess. Pretty soon, all that's left is the truth staring you in the face, but it's too late to fix what you done wrong, anyhow. Don't take the path I did, son. Bring hell on yourself a hundred-fold what anybody else could ever cause you."

The deer and potatoes were softened by the whiskey. Maurel wished Walker a good night and Jacob turned in soon after that. Despite his drunken reverie, Walker stumbled to his feet and felt his way through the darkness to the shallow side of the river. He removed his boots and waded in until his jeans flooded with a cold swirl of water. The paper glow of his skin disappeared below the surface. He let the best and worst of him flow in the gentle current. He wished the convoluted way of things would peel from his skin and float discarded downstream. He prayed to God for a chance to start over. Black water below, black sky above. Walker floated in the weightless repetition of prayer until a scream came pouring over the hill. Walker swam to shore and ran up the bank soaking wet to discover Jacob frantic and the campsite torn apart.

He charged past the smoldering fire and debris and approached Maurel's tent. The green fabric had been shredded and long strips of it dangled in the wind. Blood pooled in pockets and began to seep out. Jacob was on his knees fishing through the deflated folds of the tent. "Goddamn it, Walker, get over here and help me," he yelled. Walker knelt next to him, pulling back layers of nylon as Jacob crawled into the tent on his stomach and came out with Maurel writhing on his back, moaning and gasping for air.

"What the hell happened?" Walker asked.

Jacob leered as he held firm the bleeding side of Maurel's head. "A bear," he gasped. "Somebody left out the dinner scraps and wandered off. Where the hell were you?"

"I was swimming in the creek," he said.

"You stupid son of a bitch. What the hell is wrong with you?"

"Shut up," said Walker, a pit prying open his stomach. "What should we do?"

"The truck is two miles back that way." Jacob waved his arm in what could have been any direction in the hills at night. "We're going to have to carry him."

They lifted Maurel out of the tent and laid him on the ground. Walker pulled back torn clothing sopped with blood and did his best to identify his father's wounds. He found deep cuts on his arms and abdomen and doused them with whiskey, then he pried open Maurel's teeth and let a stream of alcohol down his gullet. Maurel flailed one of his balled fists at Jacob. They managed to hold him still and bandage his wounded arm to the front of his chest with a ripped T-shirt. Jacob brandished a buck knife and cut swatches from the tent large enough to hold Maurel. He folded each tent pole in half and threaded them through slits he made in the fabric. They grabbed their packs and Jacob slung the gun across his back. Then they lifted together. Maurel's weight sagged in the nylon strung between the two poles. Walker struggled to consult the compass that hung from his neck and set them on the path north, hoping they would come out somewhere near the truck.

The forest was uncompromisingly dark. Branches snapped at their arms. Trunks of pine wider than bodies emerged as though the darkness itself had created them. Maurel shifted erratically in his makeshift stretcher and they almost dropped him twice. Walker and Jacob tripped over rocks and lost footing on the soft ground, but they stayed on course.

Maurel flopped his head violently and groaned until he collapsed back into wayward unconsciousness. He went in and out, from the blurred sway of Jacob's back to the jungles of San Lo, carrying his companyman Billy Goat on a stretcher in the very

same fashion. His unit was reversing their position from a bunker
back to the deserted beachhead that had served as their landing
point so PFC Herl could catch a medevac home. Herl never made
it off that beach, and Maurel reckoned he would not make it out
of those woods alive.

Walker heard his father's muttering and thought either the
shock was wearing off or that a far worse condition was beginning
to take hold. His arms had grown tired. He counted the rhythm of
their steps to occupy his mind and returned to Maurel's confession-
ary words by the campfire. Never would he have believed that his
father harbored any remorse for his upbringing or for the years of
attrition to which he subjected their mother. He may not have raised
them right, but by hell he raised them. There they were carrying him
through the woods. That was more than some could say. He spoke
a prayer in his head. Whether or not he and Mercy saw this through,
he prayed that his infant sons would do for him what he was doing
now for his father. In a lot of ways, that would be enough.

His heart sank at the reminder of what he was going home
to, leaving Mercy the way he had. He would gladly suffer her ire as
long as it meant he still had a chance. Walker avoided looking at his
dear father torn open before him and railed against the unthinkable conspiracy between chance and fate, trailing off in search of
one lousy moment to himself. Well, he sure found it, he cursed.

The walk took longer than either of them had hoped. Faced
with the possibility that Maurel might not survive, Walker admitted that mending the wreckage with Mercy and truly being there
for the boys might be the only chance he had left at a family. Walker let a sob escape, one he regretted as Jacob turned his head.

"Enough," Jacob snapped. "Already before I hear you crying
I can feel your end sagging back there. Pick it up, Goddamn it.
You've got the rest of your life to be sad."

They trudged over an embankment that brought them up to level ground. Walker guessed they were clear of the deep woods, and after a few hundred yards his sweaty head was refreshed by a draft of wind that barreled up the clearing of a desolate road. When the silhouette of Jacob's Bronco emerged on the shoulder, they quickened their pace. It took more than an hour to drive the path out of the hills through the valley, the nearest hospital another forty minutes beyond that. Walker climbed in the backseat to hold Maurel as he contorted in pain. He had lost a lot of blood, his pale skin cold to Walker's touch. He held Maurel's hand and felt his grip grow loose. He yelled up to Jacob that the situation was not looking too good. Jacob hunched over the wheel and drove as fast as he could.

They were ten minutes from the highway when Maurel seized. Walker watched the road from the back when the bones in his fingers were smashed together in his father's last desperate grasp. His jeaned legs kicked against glass and steel. Jacob kept the wheel straight as his seat bucked from behind. He yelled for Walker to do something, so Walker reached into the backseat and held Maurel's head and tilted back his chin so he wouldn't choke. He was certain if he stuck his fingers in past gnashing teeth he would lose them. He was holding Maurel to keep him from falling off the seat when, just like that, a switch was flipped. Maurel stopped fighting and relaxed, every joint and muscle letting go as he grew weaker. The urgency to make it to the hospital expired with Walker's last hope that his father would survive. The least he could do for his father, he reasoned, was provide one final act of mercy. "Don't go to the hospital," he told Jacob. "Just go home."

Walker climbed on top of his father's twisted body. Maurel's eyes bulged through the ceiling of the truck and Walker caressed the side of his face, humming a song. The singing soothed Maurel and he glared around, as if the music was coming from another world. Walker hushed him and continued singing as he tightened his grip until the veins in his father's neck grew thick and desperate. Maurel arched his ribs, heaving under the weight. Walker pressed harder until the last tremors shook through his limbs, then sat back, breathing heavily. As the truck sped toward civilization, Walker gathered himself, then slid both lids over his father's eyes and whispered goodbye.

SIX

A BURNING SPIRE CAST a bright ring across the yard. Baynes and Truitts, friends, neighbors, elders, and kids gathered beside the flames and lined up at two banquet tables crowded with heaving trays of barbecue brisket and chicken, collards, beans, and cornbread. Walker dealt with the sudden rush of guests the only way he knew: by feeding them pounds of meat, filling buckets with cold bottles of beer, and lighting a big fire.

A group of children huddled in a circle at the head of the driveway. Miles, the brothers' young second cousin, captivated them with tell of a legendary mountain man who stalked the surrounding hills searching for lost children.

"He ain't no mountain man," a little girl objected, zipped tight in a pink camouflage jacket. "I hear he was a reaper, you know, like death stalkin' folks."

Miles continued in his best spooky voice. "He used to tend wheat and corn, raise up goats and a mean old mule, but disease come one year so he stopped harvesting his crop and started harvesting *people*. My brother says he walks these woods looking for people to do magic to."

"He a hoodoo?" the little girl asked.

"Don't know about all that." Miles pointed a knotted stick toward the forest. "What I do know is, when he gets tired of stalking through them trees back thar through that holler, he comes out to sleep sometimes right in this here barn." The tip of the branch scraped against the bottom of the barn door. "He can't stay in the woods as long as he used to, neither."

Another boy asked, "How come?"

"'Cause he's hundreds of years old. He has a big long beard with gray whiskers. He's ten feet tall with long fingernails and teeth sharp as razors fer eatin' kids." Miles peeked across the open crack in the barn door. "He could be sleeping in there right now…" He pushed the stick against the door and slid it open a few inches on the rollers. Two girls screamed and one of the boys yelled, "*Run!*" They scattered on divergent paths.

Malcolm and Jordan staked out chairs in the lawn beside the fire. "How long since we last sat in this spot? Some things never get old," said Malcolm. "Little Rock ain't that far, I know, but it's another world up here."

Jordan eyed his brother. "I hear you. I was in the music room looking at old photos of us as kids. At first, I was just flipping through the pages. Then I stopped on one of us right back there in the yard, and I thought, this is that same body. A lot has happened since. We've grown up, sure, but I am today what I was back then. You too. You're still the same know-it-all you ever were."

Malcolm stared into the fire. "You were in Dad's music room?"

"Even played a bit. First time that's ever happened, if you can believe it."

"Never in a million years would I have thought I'd hear you say that."

"It was just a few songs."

"Still," said Malcolm.

Jordan looked across the fire at their father and asked Malcolm if he thought Walker looked happy.

"I think he likes having everybody around like this."

"Hey, like I said, I was looking through one of the albums he's got downstairs. I never knew Dad and Uncle Jake were twins. Seems so obvious now, can't believe I didn't see it before," he said.

"Twins?"

Jordan pointed back and forth between them. "Like you and me. Idn't it strange?"

"That we didn't know, maybe. It's not that surprising, it runs in our family. Genetics."

Malcolm rolled to his feet from his chair and disappeared around the far side of the fire to find more beer. A trail of ice water sprayed across Jordan's chin as he caught the can that had been whipped at him. Malcolm plopped back in his seat and caught a fresh breath of air after a long sip. "So," he said, changing the conversation. "How did you end up in Texas? Be honest."

"I was playing down in Austin. A girl asked me to go back to San Antonio with her after I got done with the show. Well, I spent the weekend. Things fell out but I never left. That was three years ago."

"Living with a mistake after you realize you've made one can be hell." Malcolm had never heard his brother admit he had done anything wrong before. For the most part, he just figured Jordan regretted so much of what he had done over the years that coming to terms with it as a whole was too monumental a task, and expecting him to deal with any one part of his past was equally useless, too small an atonement to register. Malcolm didn't want to put his brother in an awkward position by pursuing it further, so he asked about work.

"I get put on construction when I need, make a hundred a night playing twice a week at the bar," he said.

Malcolm slapped his brother on the knee. "If you're playing so regular, you should make a go of it. Isn't that what you always wanted? What's holding you back?"

"You don't get it," Jordan replied.

"Help me get it, then."

"A couple years there weren't the best." Jordan sipped his beer and sighed. "Hell, it's been more or less shit right up until yesterday when I left Texas. I been in the grip of something these past few years. Maybe my whole life, I don't know. Sure seems that way. I left here because things were getting out of hand. I was in danger before I left, I don't know if you knew that. I was about to do something I could have never taken back, but at the last minute I knew I couldn't go through with it. I would have been a criminal the rest of my days. There was no way I was getting out without a fight, I knew that. When those guys caught up with me, I remember grabbing the sides of my head, clenching my teeth, trying to outlast the blows, thinking, 'This is it.' They took turns wailing on me and stomping my head 'til they cracked my skull round back here and knocked out my hearing. I don't remember much. There's this mute haze of jeans and boots dancing in headlights, the dirt soaking up my blood as it poured out of me. Then the dust cleared. I wasn't dead, so I told myself I would be all right. I got out of there and never came back. It couldn't have gone any other way.

"I floated around for a while—East Coast, California, Mexico. Wherever I woke up, each day was worse than the last. By the end of that year I was in and out of drunk tanks, did a stretch in jail. That sobered me up long enough to know something was calling out for me. From a place deeper than bone, Malcolm. A force pulling me into the dark. I tried to make it stop, but it didn't come from one place, it came from all over, every inch of my body. I couldn't run from it, neither. Wherever I went, there it was. Drinking ain't a fraction as bad as what's calling out for me, brother. I used to get so tired and think it wouldn't be so bad if I just gave in to what it wants. I had nothing to my name and no pride left to defend, but I got wise. Been keeping my head low and staying out of the way, as of late." Jordan pointed to the island of blue engulfing his left eye. "A few exceptions, of course."

"Looks like you're healing up nicely." Malcolm's face broke with laughter and they each took a drink.

"You know, being home this time, I don't feel so bad." Jordan sounded surprised. "And you're getting married," he said, as though reminding himself. "I have a lot of love for you guys, I wasn't ready to accept that before."

The brothers reached out and hugged in the night air. "You've got me weeping over here," Malcolm said, sniffling. Jordan tightened his grip and wouldn't let him pull free. Malcolm wrenched back and sat upright, straightening his shirt.

One of Walker's old friends, a bearded, glassy-eyed octogenarian named Fellows, raised a plea across the lawn for Walker to play a song for those who had gathered. He offered to fetch a guitar from inside, which seemed to only put Walker out. He made a hushing motion, lowering his palm to quiet his friends. The fire crackled and Malcolm and Jordan listened to their father's papery voice lilt its way through the heavy night. Elizabeth stood beside her mother and aunts, admiring Walker's song. Malcolm watched his fiancée as she stood surrounded by her kin and was reminded of the first time he saw her on the UNC campus, an intelligent, unhampered beauty. He knew instantly he was in love with her. Out of instinct, he followed her to class, and did so the same exact way for weeks. Even though he was only in his junior year, he was sure enough to know how rare a gift their affection was, and he resolved not to let the opportunity of loving her pass him by. Lucky for him, she felt the same.

The hymnal "Beautiful Home" carried and others joined in the song while Malcolm remained lost in reverie. He had not heard Walker's worn tenor in so long, not counting the few times he caught it playing on the radio. A late-night country station in Little Rock would sometimes play *In Low Company*, a record bluegrass aficionados held in particularly high regard. His voice was softer and much more fragile in person.

"You're not listening to a word I am saying, are you?" Jordan knew Malcolm was off someplace else, so he leaned forward in his chair to tap Lester Fellows as he passed. "Hey, Lester, do you know if my uncle Jake is coming to the wedding?" Jordan watched as the old man furrowed his brow.

"Who's that now? Jacob?" he asked. "You boys sure been gone a long time. Walker and Jake ain't spoke since I don't know when. Longer than should stand between kin, y'ask me. They fell out over something way back."

"Do you know what about?" Jordan asked.

"That thar's between your dad and Jake." Lester paused and leaned down. "Wouldn't ask too many questions, son." He walked off past the fire.

Jordan lit a smoke, mired by what little he knew about his family. In the years before, he would not have cared, but it was as though he was beginning to see things for the first time and now it was getting to him. He breathed smoke and fought the uncomfortable inertia that tossed him back and forth between those thoughts.

Malcolm hit him in the leg. "You going to see Leah?"

Jordan stuck his thumb and forefinger in his eyes. Smoke curling from his mouth, he let out a groan.

"Jesus, you are one dramatic son of a bitch," said Malcolm.

The fire cracked as someone tossed new wood on top of the pile.

"Well?" Malcolm reiterated.

"Well what?"

"Do you intend to see her?"

"Fuck no." Jordan swilled his beer as though washing a foul taste from his mouth.

Leah Fayette was Jordan's last girl before he left Newton County. They had not seen each other since the night he left. She never knew it, but on his way out of town, when he was beaten and bloody, Jordan sat in his car outside her house, watching her move in unison with the bold contour of a man behind white drapes.

A short, fiery brunette, Leah had an ivy-wrapped banner tattooed across the front of her chest with the name of her older brother, Stephen, and the day, month, and year he was cut in half by an IED on the road to Tikrit. Jordan always considered her mean spirit a necessary if clumsy and volatile defense. Leah made the easy mistake of confusing violence with love. Sometimes that left little room for understanding a man doing less than his best to love her. While Jordan was doing his best to be decent, she ran around setting fires, and when she came around, brought down by her trail of ruin and seeking out affection, Jordan was nowhere to be found. In the years they spent together, he never asked her to explain herself, not once. Jordan wished he'd done right by her, but they were wrong for each other from the beginning.

Provoked by the question, he was gripped by the prospect of possibly facing the one person who knew the ugly truth about him, as much as any one person could. He swore off seeing her and emptied the last of his beer. He told Malcolm he was heading out to meet some people for drinks and that he should come along. Malcolm wanted to explain how tired he was, but he knew the only result that would come from such a lame excuse would be endless mockery, and he didn't have the energy for that. Plus, he hadn't spent a night in town with his brother in the last decade, so reluctantly he agreed. Jordan jumped up out of the lawn chair. "That's what I'm talking about," he exclaimed, forcing a high-five that stung Malcolm's palm.

Jordan and Elizabeth hung from each other's shoulders as they walked into Silver Bar, Jordan leading them to the back corner where his friends Harrell, Russ, and Baron Fuchs rose around a table with beers in hand.

Baron, who years ago Jordan understandably nicknamed Fucks, was a ginger the size of a refrigerator. His big smile moved toward Malcolm as he crushed the wind out of him with a hug. Harrell wore a dingy T-shirt and jeans, face shaded beneath the worn curve of a baseball cap. Harrell and Jordan were inseparable for the first half of their lives and felt like no time had passed since then. Russ greeted his old friend and went out of his way to ignore Malcolm. Tall and thin with ratty black hair, Russ had one sleeve pinned above the crease at his elbow. He lost the arm while logging most of the unprotected timber in the county when he was only nineteen. Prescribed Oxy after the accident, he sank into a concentrated spiral of eradication. Nobody saw much of Russ after that.

Elizabeth reached out and shook Russ's hand. Her breath caught in her chest unexpectedly when the fibrous, meandering scar that ran from the back of his scalp to his elbow came into her view. Baron broached the silence by complimenting Malcolm on marrying such a fine girl. They all took their seats and caught up in quick bursts of banter until the bartender brought two pitchers of cold beer and recognized Jordan. "If it ain't the Patron Saint of good ol' fuckin' Misery. Didn't know you was back," Johnny, the bartender, said. "Thought I'd have heard the sirens."

"Laying low, Johnny. Real low. But my dear brother here is getting married, and you know we can't let that go off without an occasion." Jordan pointed at Malcolm with his beer.

Johnny reached across the table and tossed Malcolm's shoulder back and forth. "You hitching this one here?" Elizabeth weathered his gaze with grace. "My lord," he said, straightening his appearance. "What have I been doing with my life?" Laughter crossed the table as Johnny hustled back to the front. A few minutes later, he returned with a tray of shots and more congratulations.

"I should get married more often." Malcolm hoisted his whiskey. Elizabeth hid away behind her glass, red from all the attention. As they drank and caught up, Malcolm could not help but notice Russ staring at him. He looked away, but Russ persisted, setting Malcolm in his angry, harrowed glare.

In so many words, Russ blamed Malcolm for the loss of his arm. Russ had worked on a logging crew that was cutting in the woods a few miles from the Bayne house when Russ ripped into a pine with an iron rod spiked through the trunk. The chain spun from his saw, sending the jagged metal teeth clear through his arm and embedding them in the back of his head. He was lucky he wasn't killed, but Russ didn't see it that way. Nurses drew his blood at the hospital and his toxicology came back positive for alcohol, opiates, and methamphetamine. Malcolm was in his first year as junior clerk for Ringgold Insurance, the same company that denied Russ a settlement for the result of his accident. Russ's employer refused to file a compensation claim and fired him as he lay in the hospital bed recovering from a series of surgeries that left him bankrupt. Russ had greater demons to fight, but he never forgave Malcolm for being involved.

Jordan headed out to smoke and saw a young woman wavering on a bench by the front door. She hit her head on the armrest and nearly fell at Jordan's feet. Johnny yelled from behind the bar that she should call a friend or he would be happy to call her a police cruiser. She picked up the falling weight of her head and somehow managed to dial a cell phone that she mashed into her cheek. "Come get me," the girl slurred, "or they're gonna make me take a cruise." The voice on the other end tried to ascertain where she was. "I'm on a bench," she said, loud and slow, as though she could not hear her own words. The girl reached out for Jordan's pant leg as he walked past. There was a time when just that would have been enough, and he would have woke beside her the next morning, the two squinting at each other, trying to remember how they got there, but he kicked her away as though sloughing off a small animal.

Johnny the bartender joined Jordan outside. They stood on the curb blowing smoke and rolling gravel beneath their feet.

"That's great about your brother," said Johnny. "Girl's stunning."

"Tell me about it. Speaking of brothers, Adam still around?" Jordan asked.

"In a manner of speaking." Johnny blew a heavy breath. "Crashed his bike about five months ago in the hills on 540. It was dark, started raining, went over the rail straight into nothing."

"Jesus, man. I'm sorry."

"He ain't dead," said Johnny. "Sum' bitch is laid up at home smoking weed and playing Xbox. Thought the accident would wake him up—boy, was I wrong."

He kicked the small stones and Jordan him asked if he was going to the wedding Saturday.

"Wasn't invited," he said.

"Well, you are now," Jordan told him. "If you're not busy Thursday night, come to the bachelor party. Should be a time."

Johnny nodded.

A beat-up red Civic swung into the lot and stopped short at the curb. The driver's side door shot open and a woman stepped out in a mess of jingling bracelets and wild brown hair. Leah Fayette took a few hard steps toward the door, but when she saw Jordan the rhythm of her heels clicked to a stop. Johnny flicked his cigarette and ran back inside the bar.

"So, it's true," said Leah, looking anywhere but ahead.

"Whatever you're going to say—"

"I don't intend to say nothin'. You know what? Fuck you. Don't preempt me, you don't get to anticipate what I am going to say. As far as I am concerned you are a figment, a sad ghost. Go find someone else to haunt."

Jordan had no other recourse but to remain silent and light another cigarette. He offered her one, but Leah stormed away, then roared back a moment later and lit her own.

Jordan asked how she was doing.

"What?" Leah replied.

"I mean, what are you doing here? Are you, you know, meeting someone?"

"Wouldn't you love to know." She worked to retain her composure. "I came to pick up my friend. Apparently she's shitfaced."

Jordan recalled the girl on the bench but didn't see the point in mentioning her. "My brother's getting married," he said.

"Good for him," Leah said. "No, seriously," she added, peering at a passing car. "I always liked Malcolm. Tell him I said congratulations."

"Do you want to—" Jordan mumbled into his chest. "I mean, you are welcome to, if that's something that would, um, interest you."

Leah drew smoke, studying her phantom. She stepped closer to him. "We have a long way to go before that would ever be a reality."

To have Leah that close incensed him and he took in what about her had retained its dark, warped shape and in what ways, in outer appearance anyway, she had changed. Ultimately, though, he found himself contemplating how she had remained withdrawn after all these years. "I read somewhere that we make our own reality," he told her.

Leah threw her smoke and headed inside.

The group stood around the trunks of their cars moving from congratulations to goodbyes, Malcolm repeating the logistics of their big day while Elizabeth brushed off compliments and stored new numbers in her phone. In the commotion, Russ, rudderless from a number of drinks, leaned close to Malcolm and whispered beneath his breath.

Malcolm asked loudly for him to repeat himself.

Russ stood apart from the rest of the group, dead-eyed and morose. "I said, it takes a bitch to marry a bitch."

Jordan felt the heat rise between them. He knew his brother was deciding whether or not it was a good idea to beat Russ into the pavement right there in front of Elizabeth. In an effort to defuse the situation, Jordan did what came to mind first and tripped himself onto to the ground, scattering the contents of his pockets across the pavement. "You're just going to stand there after tripping a guy, Elizabeth? That's low, even for you. Come on, help a poor wretch." She laughed and Harrell leaned down and helped her haul Jordan back to his feet.

At the next bar, they clanked down a round of shots and Malcolm joked that Elizabeth made Jordan behave himself. She did have a calming effect on him, something more than manners.

"So, Jordan," Elizabeth said with a drunk tongue. "Why did you really go to jail?"

"Lizzie," Malcolm protested.

"No, its fine, she's family now," Jordan assured him. "For being an idiot," he told Elizabeth. "I went to jail for being an idiot."

"Yes, but what does that *mean?*"

"It means one night I had myself about twenty drinks, give or take, and went on a bender that ended with my truck plowed through the front of a nursing home in Alamosa, Colorado. The cab was sitting at an angle on part of a steel door frame and a bunch of smashed drywall, so I climbed out and wandered inside. Apparently, I found a service kitchen and cooked up a bunch of tortillas for the residents of the nursing home, who were curious to know who was making all the racket. The cop told me that I was under the impression I was making a late-night snack at my apartment in La Veta, over an hour away. A nurse and a couple of officers found me with some elderly folks in their slippers and nightgowns laughing about God knows what, eating tortillas and having a ball. When the police cuffed me and took me out, they all waved at me and shouted, 'Goodbye, Jordie! Hope you have fun in jail!'"

Elizabeth could not contain her laughter and spit her drink on the table. Malcolm was unable to read his brother, but the laughter spread to Jordan as Malcolm sopped up the mess with a handful of napkins. Elizabeth apologized.

"No need to be sorry," Jordan told her. "It's good to talk about these things." He couldn't get to the end of his sentence before both of them were overcome again like a couple of children with an inside joke. She asked him to keep going with his story, and Jordan caught his breath. "Well, prison is a pallid hell I'd just as soon not discuss. When I got out, I lived in a little valley at the foot of Blanca Peak. Not very far from the jail, even. You'd think

I'd have wanted to get as far away from that place as possible, but I was empty. A blank slate, no fight left in me. There was nowhere else to go. I just wandered outside the gate and thought it was pretty, so I stayed. Big sky, quiet nights. Didn't know a soul. Got work hauling steel girders off the loaders that came up the pass. In the summer I slept outside. Didn't even have a guitar. Hard work and a little anonymity will do a lot to heal a person."

They ordered another round from the waitress, and Jordan noticed a group pointing in their direction from the bar. A girl hopped off her stool and made her way to their table, two men at her side as she approached hard and tough. "How's bout paying your bill and movin' on out of here?"

"Just ordered another round, actually. Thinking of staying a while," Jordan said, lamenting being seated on the inside of the booth.

"Maybe you don't hear so well," she spewed. Jordan recognized her fetal-alcohol drawl as the same woman who recited the dire warning to his voicemail before he came back.

"Hey, fuckface, she's talking to you," one of the guys said.

Before Jordan could do anything about it, he watched as his brother rose to his feet, gripped the neck of the man closest to him, and slammed his forehead off the corner of the table. Drinks jumped and leaked rivers of booze. The ketchup broke and salt and pepper shakers rolled onto the floor where the man fell bleeding. The girl covered her mouth in shock. Malcolm moved with his fist cocked toward the other one, who flinched and backed away, then he stared the shivering girl dead in the eyes. A big bouncer grabbed Malcolm from behind, but not before he kicked the man on the ground once more, forcing a gasp from his lungs. The bouncer corralled Elizabeth and Jordan together with Malcolm and forced them out the door. The tough girl sobbed on her knees, cradling the bleeding man's head in her lap. "Get up," she pleaded. "Baby, please, get up."

The three drove the winding road home in silence. It took a while for the adrenaline coursing through Malcolm to wane. As Jordan drove, Malcolm stared out the back window and fought the undeniable truth that a small part of holding that man down and pounding his flesh felt good. Something about it felt natural to him. He had not apologized to Elizabeth, who sat horrified in the passenger seat. Jordan kept his eyes on the road and contained his obvious excitement. Finally, his enthusiasm wore down Elizabeth past her limit. "That's enough, Jordan. It's not funny," she said.

"No it's not," he said, smiling. "It's just, well, usually that's me." Jordan looked at his brother in the rearview mirror. "You stuck up for me," he said, exaggerating big deep breaths, as though refreshed by his brother's valor. "My stars," he joked, hitting Elizabeth on the leg. She returned a fuming specter that threatened to exceed mere displeasure and careened instead straight toward eternal judgment. Malcolm knew that look, though he hadn't seen it that intense in a long time. Jordan leered away from her general direction and kept his eyes glued to the road the rest of the way home. When the car pulled into the driveway, Elizabeth got out and slammed the door.

"Don't worry about her, she'll be all right," Jordan assured Malcolm, still sulking in the back. "How you doing? Still all tuned up?"

Malcolm nodded.

"Yeah, that's natural," said Jordan. "It'll pass."

Malcolm squinted out the back window, searching the molasses sky. "Natural," he scoffed. There was no such thing.

SEVEN

ANDRIDGE GRIEVES' EYES GLOWED as he gazed into the stone hold. The old one reclined in a hide-back chair, the confines of which he far outsized. His lean, wizened relief looked as though it had been chipped from the side of a mountain, a countenance that had given birth to his many nicknames—Hill Devil, Shadow Hat, Weatherhands, the Carrollton Creeper. Most rumors went out with each generation of schoolchildren telling stories, sometimes about a reclusive hill dweller, a ghost turned manifest, other times a child-killing hermaphrodite who lurked at the dead ends of streets, stalking the foggy hollers that grew deep beyond local creeks. Those children became adults, and whether they ended up teaching at the schoolhouse, bagging groceries at the local store, or favoring cheap booze and strong pills as passable diversions from the misery of poverty, they all continued to talk, trading ghost stories and superstition for hearsay and gossip about everyone who came around the corner.

Legend placed Andridge about town between the market and Eberle's feed store and the deteriorated lanes in Felson Woods, a desolate expanse that ran against the far southern edge of the Bayne property. Edna Jackson, a teacher at the elementary, told anyone that would listen about the time she crossed Grieves on the forest road that led to the electric station. It was late, almost dusk. At first she mistook him for strange weather, on account of the gray day. When a strong wind blew she swore it tore right through his overalls, jacket and all. She thought he might have been approaching her, invisible like an apparition, and cowered out of terror. When she looked back, he was gone.

Other more nefarious actors used to come around. Magicians, seers, myth hunters seeking tall tales and local lore, motivated by boredom or a small desire for profit. They thought Andridge was a regular boogeyman, a myth and nothing more, even though they had come to search for him or else prove he never existed. Inevitably, one or two did come face to face with Andridge, and upon learning he was real they fled down roads of solace and locked themselves in cabins and motel rooms muttering about the devil.

Obediah Cob, his partner and oldest friend, was a fully grown homunculus whose origins were nothing short of a mystery. He imagined his poor Missourian parents giving him up for adoption at the turn of the last century, but Andridge once suggested that an alchemist could have conjured him from a meld of earthen substances. Semen and ewe blood, sunstone, willow sap, sputum, and manure. Cob was aware of such attempts throughout history and remained wary of their success, though he respected the depths of the dream that made up the world.

He was half Andridge's age and nowhere near possessed the powers he did, but Cob had peculiar abilities his own. His one true gift was his ability to speak the language of everything in the world—human and animal languages, plants and elder trees, shadows, aural entities, ancient ghosts, and the newly dead. Andridge suspected these capabilities upon their meeting in a Missouri antique shop in the spring of 1919. He had stopped in to inquire about a Vauclusian mirror that had made it out of France before the war.

The owner of the shop was a stout German whose brutish tone drove Andridge away from purchasing the mirror. Frustrated to lose such a lucrative sale, especially in times as lean as those, the owner stormed behind the counter, cursing as he slammed boxes around. Andridge was unable to understand German, so at first he thought the man was cursing to himself, but as he walked to the front of a showroom cluttered with relics and choked with dust, a peculiar little man came into view and Andridge realized the owner was berating him. Though it was unintelligible, it sounded like a nasty tirade, one the little man shrugged off as though he was all too used to it, before he replied to the hostile shop owner in his own calm, distinctive German.

Andridge pressed himself over a cloudy glass case and waved to get their attention. "Excuse me, sir. May I speak with you a moment?" he called to Cob.

The German hobbled out, apologizing for his dimwitted employee, but Andridge interrupted him. "No, you misunderstand. I wish to talk with that dimwitted employee, not you." Cob snickered as he came to the front of the counter and stepped atop a red leather case. Andridge asked his name.

"Cob," he said. "Obediah Cob."

"Have you been working here long, Obediah?"

"A couple months. Told me I wouldn't be hired anywhere else besides the carnival, so I should appreciate the opportunity he has given me. Pays a pittance, fancies himself ecumenical, but he's just full of Protestant nonsense. Honest, I think he likes having me around. He needs someone to yell at."

"Your German is very good, he can't hate that. How many languages would you say you know?"

"A great many, indeed," Cob said.

Andridge looked him up and down, enamored by the young man. "Tell you what, Obediah. How would you like to come work for me?"

"Doing what?" Cob asked.

"A great many things," Andridge said. "I am getting on in years, see, and could use someone to assist with my work—an *assistant*. I quite like the sound of that. You seem of right ilk and, if I may be frank, in possession of talents that are going to waste here. You would be praised, not berated. Your pay would more than increase. What do you say?"

The two exchanged a long, studious glance. Cob returned to the back room to work his coat over his shoulders and fish a rare trinket from a box below his desk, a small solid gold casting of an eagle that he fit into the bag hanging from his shoulder. He turned to the shop owner and said in German, "May you die alone among forgotten treasures," and walked through the door that Andridge held open for him.

Obediah returned to the cabin and Andridge asked where he had been. "I followed the Bayne boys," he said. "They got in a tussle and were ejected from a local establishment."

"That Jordan has a mean streak to him yet," Andridge observed.

"Actually, it was Malcolm. I was surprised myself." Cob laid a tray on the table next to Andridge's chair that held fixings for drinks. He pulled two cigarettes from a pack, lit both with a gold lighter, and handed one to Andridge. He stood at the side of the table preparing gin sodas. The fire cracked, ice hit glass, and cocktails fizzed as they discussed the brothers' arrival. Cob voiced his concern. "I know you said Jordan is the one who has been chosen, but do you really think he could be a killer? I'm not sure I see it."

"He is beginning to emerge from the shadow of his father. They are practically spitting images of each other," said Andridge.

"Walker Bayne was unruly and arrogant in his time, too. Only he was much better at hiding it. Jordan has been fitted for violence. His mother's passed, he's estranged from his brother and hates his father. I would say it's a safe bet."

"You were the one who said never to work off an assumption. Remember where that got us last time? You were forced to intervene."

"Who said I was assuming?" asked Andridge, sipping his drink.

"We do not yet know who will be responsible for the rite."

"What do we know about Malcolm?"

"Compared to Jordan? He's been a pillar of order his entire life. Good career, owns his home, genuinely loves his soon-to-be wife. From what I have seen, he can be cold, but not enough to kill. He has no reason. The risk would be too great. Too much to lose, nothing to gain. That's why he is good with insurance. He is excellent at gauging the outcome of a situation. His actions have never been as severe as his brother's, nor as unpredictable. He has been a watcher his whole life. He is born from water."

"He doesn't have to have a reason, it only has to happen," Andridge stressed. "He may not be as docile as we think."

Cob sniped his cigarette. "Jordan and Walker are alike," he conceded. "But Malcolm and Jacob? It doesn't add up. Jacob was far more violent. He killed a Klansman, if you recall."

Andridge let out a dry laugh, troubled by a cough. "No, of course they're not the same."

"We have been at this so long that when we don't have a good feeling, like this one here, when these boys been gone a decade and now all of a sudden they are both back, the one getting married and the other I don't know what—making amends, I guess—and we have not seen them or kept up with them the entire time, we don't know their true natures, and if we don't know what it's in their nature to do, then we don't know what they're capable of," Cob argued. "We could have easily missed something."

"Keep an eye out, then," Andridge told him.

Cob wiggled his empty in the air. "Want another?"

Andridge handed over his jar. "Do the blind see God?"

Malcolm curled his knuckles along the stock of a Browning T-Bolt, tightened his jaw, and pulled the trigger, blowing his shoulders and neck back from the puff of gray that danced in front of him. A small audience of young nieces, nephews, and cousins stood at a safe distance clutching their ears, faces fattened with surprise. An assortment of rifles, pistols, and revolvers were laid out on the picnic table—the Browning, a Remington compact, an M&P .40, Ruger 9 millimeter, and two .22 pistols that were perfect for young ones eager to shoot.

Twenty years before, Walker taught him in that same spot on a cold November morning. The winter sun spread weakly across the trees. He remembered the lessons of his father and repeated them to his captive young audience. "Never point a gun at another human being," he said.

"Unless you want them to die?" one of them asked.

"Unless you want them to die," Malcolm repeated. "Spread your stance, like this." Walker had jostled Malcolm's leg a little too hard and his sneaker slid on the frozen grass. He dropped the gun and it hit the ground, firing off to the right. Walker dove out of the way, smacked his son's crying face, then pulled Malcolm out of the mud and into his arms. The gun he had dropped was the Remington compact. Malcolm loved that gun. He walked over to the table and picked it up. "Which of y'all wants to shoot?" The kids rushed around him and Malcolm had them line up so they could fire into the woods.

Mary and Elizabeth sipped coffee in the kitchen and listened to the light cracks erupt between cheers from the children. Walker in his slippered walk snuck up behind the two backs huddled in front of the window.

Elizabeth leapt and held her hand to the base of her chest. "Jesus," she breathed.

"Nope, still waitin' on Him," Walker joked.

"Just the man I wanted to see. I have a few questions about the ceremony." Mary jumped right in. "Who is going to be here at six on Saturday to instruct the caterers for setup? Someone's got to be here to sign for FedEx at eight, too. Are you going to be home, or should I have them leave the package by the downstairs door?"

Walker was barely paying attention.

"Hello? Are you listening?" Mary asked. "It's priority. Someone has to sign for it."

"One of the perks of having this wedding in my own backyard is that I have to walk from here to about there to attend. Ain't I footing the bill? I don't need to hear about it every minute. People're around," he said. "Take care of it."

Mary shook her head. "Get out of here, then," she said. "Go on, go."

Walker smirked as he shuffled past, happy to oblige.

Young Miles sat on a picnic table, swinging his legs as he pushed his small fingers into the grooves one of the rifles. The wood stock was faded, scratched with smooth lines, and the steel around the barrel was tarnished. "What about this one, Malcolm? It looks old," Miles said.

Malcolm picked it up by the military-issue strap. "This is a Japanese T-5, a knockoff of the M1." None of them knew what that meant. "This rifle was used in World War Two." The remote age of that fabled conflict prompted their intrigue and immediately they wanted to shoot it.

"No, you can't shoot it," said Malcolm. "This thing is bigger than most of you, you'd go flying right back into the house." Malcolm laughed and held it high as they reached for it anyway. "Fine," Malcolm said. "Y'all search through that box, see if you can find some thirty-aught-six ammo. If you find some, maybe we'll see if this thing still works."

Their small hands dove into the box. Nine-year-old Mary Ann counted her ability to read among her talents that exalted her above the rest of the children. She sat on top of the picnic table, reading the numbers printed on the boxes of bullets. "Here it is!" she yelled, handing the box to Malcolm. He tried loading the magazine, but the brass shells were too long to fit in the clip. Jordan walked out of the house and Malcolm asked if he knew what ammunition the T-5 took.

Jordan peered into the recesses of the rifle. "It's Japanese," he said, examining it. "Probably takes some fucked-up caliber. It's not in the box?" he asked. "Did you check in the barn?"

"Can you do it? I'm watching the kids."

Jordan gave him a look.

"Just check the barn," Malcolm insisted.

The cavernous breadth of the barn enveloped a car that sat beneath a cloth which Jordan folded back, revealing the faded brown '74 Eldorado exalted on blocks of cinder like a shrine in the middle of the floor. Two large tool chests massed the far wall beside a workbench caked with grease. Jordan ducked under the jack beam that held the hayloft overhead and entered a side room with tall, packed shelves. He pulled a couple of boxes free from their imprints of dust and stacked them at his side until he spotted the distinct metallic green of a foot locker that was lodged far in the back. He grabbed hold of the tarnished buckle and slid it forth to the edge of the wood. He pulled the leather straps through the locks at each side. The clasps on the front were rusted shut, but Jordan strained until they flew open.

He unearthed the personal effects of his grandfather Maurel's tour in the Pacific—medals, a ration tin, knife, official papers, telegrams, and letters. He dug out a munitions case and found the oddly calibered .707 rounds for the T-5. The machined cylinders were cool between his fingers. There was a black-and-white photograph that Maurel had taken of Walker and Jacob as children, fidgeting in their Sunday best in front of the same barn where he now stood. There were telegrams from his wife and a few letters from Maurel's brother, Casey, stuffed into a leather satchel.

Jordan squatted against the wall and read his grandfather's letters. Apparently, Maurel found the tropics to be murder—clothes soaked with sweat, soggy feet festering in their boots, skin hived and malarial, no relief to be found from the fire of the air. Elephantine beetles got in Maurel's tent one night and crawled out with dime-sized tokens of his flesh held in their huge, mechanical jaws. He wrote to Casey when he couldn't sleep, which was most nights. He kept the letters tucked away in his pack until he found a way to mail them all at once. Men clung to any constancy in order to survive the crushing alienation of foreign skies, unending gun fire, and the ferocious shells that hit all around when it was least expected. Maurel did his best to eat, shit, and pray as though death were not constantly lining him in its sights.

The hot season was not much different than summer in the Ozarks. Heat flooded the valleys in molten waves and would not lift for days. They would march at night and stop by noon. They would drink tea in the shade, beer at the creek, and pass white whiskey around the fire. Some of the boys sang songs that reminded them of home while Maurel laid back and looked up at the sky, daydreaming about the girls in a nearby village. Though he was soon to ship out, Jordan was surprised to read Maurel telling Casey that he would not be coming back home. *Because of what happened to Pa?* Casey asked in his last letter, a reply that went unanswered. *If that's what you're getting on, Marl, you needn't worry. That's all blowed over now, I swear. It's like none of it ever happened.*

EIGHT

1938—THE MINE COLLAPSE

Casey Bayne was on his way fishing when he came upon a tarp that had been camouflaged with detritus from the surrounding hill. He drew it back and uncovered an underground cavern where a homemade still piped sour steam into pure moon juice. He grabbed a single Mason jar and climbed back out, then held the clear liquor up to the sun and laughed.

Casey made sure to fix up the site to erase any evidence of his being there before continuing on to Bethlehem Creek. He sopped along the muddy bank until he found a spot, rolled his pant legs, sank in his scrawny shins, and cast his jig for catfish and perch. That night, Casey brought home a stinking bucket of fish and handed the half-drunk jar to his brother, Maurel.

"Whosever rig that is won't be too happy when they find someone's been pinching their product. Liable to keep an eye out, Case."

"Covered it up like I wasn't ever there," said Casey. "Gone wait a week, let suspicions clear. I want you to go back there with me and together we'll grab as much of that dew as we can get our hands on. We'll go at night, one trip only, whatever fits in the wagon." Casey wavered where he stood, giddy and drunk.

A rarified vapor snaked from the mouth of the jar and nearly blistered the whites off of Maurel's eyes. He shrank back, fumbling to screw the lid on. "That's the stupidest idea I have ever heard," he said.

"I know it is, that's why I need your help." Casey wrestled the jar back from Maurel and sucked a huge gulp off the lip that knocked him back into the rickety chair, searing his mouth. He pushed both eyes closed with his fists, like someone had just dropped a lit coal on the back of his brain.

"I don't want to cause you any distress here, Case, but I'm gonna need you to think real hard for just a second."

Casey splayed over the table, nodding.

"There are only two ways this plays out," Maurel explained. "That spot belongs to some hiller, maybe a farmer—could be an honest one at that—and that honest farmer's out of work like everyone else round here and maybe, Case, that still and those jars are all he's got to his name. To earn a living and feed his family. Maybe he's fine guarding 'em with his life, 'cause you take that away and heck, maybe he won't give a damn to shoot you right there. That's the better option of the two."

"Yeah, what's the other, then," Casey slurred.

Maurel stood from the table and raked his features in a sobering draw. "Who you been doing your best to keep clear of, down the end of the road past Tremble's Farm?"

"Who, Dunny?" asked Casey, wary.

Maurel hauled a five-pound bag of potatoes from the floor of the pantry and landed it on the counter. He flicked a slit in the burlap, a few potatoes fell out, and he scrubbed the dirt away in the basin. "That's right," he said. "Dunny McShay, whose brother you beat near to death last summer."

"He'd been woopin' on Genie!" Casey yelled. "Beat on ar lil' sister'n believe that's what's comin'."

"That boy deserved it, no doubt," Maurel reasoned, "but now his brother and the rest of them want you deader than shit."

Casey tossed a pinch of tobacco over a creased paper, fastened the roller, and torched the fat end with a flame.

"If that still out there don't belong to some poor cabbage fucker, I bet my right pocket it belongs to the McShay gang. If it's part of one of their rackets, then they got others, and that means they're watching them around the clock." Maurel did his best to make some sense, but he could already tell it wasn't going to take.

Their sister Genie came up the back holding a basket of apples and onions. She was tall and thin as a poke. Her fair complexion showed off her ease of spirit and constant joy, which invigorated anyone lucky enough to find themselves in her company. She put the basket on the counter, drifted by the stove, raised herself up on her toes, and kissed Maurel on the cheek.

"Hello there, brother," she said, glimpsing the potatoes. "Mm, I can't wait to eat, I'm jus' about starved."

It was that irrepressible shine his sister lost for a while when she was caught under the yoke of the McShay boy. He smiled at Genie, glad she had her glow back. Their mother, Eleanora, was not too far behind. She came through the house and shooed Maurel away from her counter. "We eat in one hour," she declared, producing a wrap of butcher's paper that all of them eyed. She unfolded it to reveal pink cuts of pork, which she sprinkled with salt and crushed peppercorn.

Maurel and Casey tried to fit through the small back door at the same time, their bodies wedged against each other, and Casey spoke low to his brother. "I don't care about that McShay bastard nor no damn hiller," he said. "Tomorrow night I am robbing that still."

———

The vibrant moon was dampened by a cover of clouds that gave the night a soft, pervasive illumination, like a high-powered bulb diffused by a heavy shade. Maurel was already tense from his brother's criminal aspirations and found the atmosphere of the night foreboding. They had borrowed their father Zuriel's diesel wagon and drove until the road ended. Maurel killed the heavy grumble of the engine, hopped from the truck, and set out with Casey along the creek bed.

He followed his brother through the dense brush over mud and water that ran shallow across roots and stones. Casey's gait disintegrated into the trees and left Maurel far enough back to lose sight of the ratty white shirt and oily chestnut locks that swayed between his shoulders. Maurel stomped along, realizing Casey had no idea where he was taking them. Maurel was frustrated further that, because they were supposed to be on a mission of stealth, he could not raise his voice a piss above a whisper to find out where Casey had gone.

A rustle rose in the brush to his left. Maurel pinioned with a punch at the ready, but when he turned, the tread of his boot slipped in the mud and he was laid flat on his chest. The lower half of his body was pulled into the creek and he craned his neck to see Casey slapping his knee, laughing like a moron.

"I found it," Casey said. "Not five minutes that way through them trees." He pointed ahead into the dark. "Come on, let's get you up." He gripped Maurel's wet shirt and pulled him to his feet. He found the tarp and drew it back, exposing neatly stacked rows of precious, incubating shine. Before ducking below the messing, Maurel looked around. Wind sweetened the air, hushed the trees, and sang in the creek. He gripped the jerry-rigged skeleton of four-by-fours for support and lowered himself into the hole.

"Wow," said Maurel. "You weren't kidding." He ran his thumb on the seam of messy welds that joined the cap arm to the base of the tank. The bottom of the still was shored up with dry quarters of wood, like a hearth.

Casey rubbed his hands together and whistled. "There is a wheelbarrow over here," he said. "It's small, but it should do the trick."

They took turns laying the filled jars on their sides until they were stacked eight wide and four deep. Maurel told Casey they were full and could not fit anymore. Casey paused in his tracks with two jars planted in each palm. A tortured look of disappointment and half-wit ingenuity screwed his face in two directions. He placed one of the jars back on the shelf, then popped the clasp on the other and swallowed three difficult mouthfuls. His body coughed in protest, but not before he did it again, getting down most of the jar in the time it took Maurel to look on in awe and then convince him to stop.

The barrow load was heavy and slid over in the mud but they managed to wheel it all the way back to the Ford. The jars fit on the slatted bed just fine. Casey pulled his long strands of hair back and paced in the dirt, boozy with adrenaline. "I wanna go back," he kept repeating. "There's at least four more hauls left and we only got one. Come on with it, Marl, it's our only shot." But Maurel would not hear a word. He secured the head of their haul with rope and snapped the tailgate shut.

"You better get, 'cause I'm leaving either way."

A few miles down the only road out, headlights came up from behind. Maurel saw the two yellow beams continue to wander around each switchback and swerve past every bend. He rolled down the driver's side window and glanced over the edge of the road, down tumbling shelves of loose rock and scattered trees. The aged truck hummed past two forks and came to a four-cornered stop. The right went to town and straight led to a state road that served as a local timber and mining corridor that met with the highway, so Maurel cut a hard left and continued on a desolate dirt road that rose and fell with the shallow slopes of the hills.

Their house came into view as they flew past Tremble's Farm. Maurel slowed to turn on the horse road that ran adjacent to the house. As he did, the commotion raised their father from his bed. Zuriel ran to the window and parted the curtain to watch his own truck kick a trail of dust through the woods. As his truck sped off, another one appeared, two men crouched in back of the bed hollering commands at the driver. The engines roared into the forest. Zuriel buttoned his gray thermal and rustled in the closet for his shotgun. He handed it to Eleanora, who sat up in bed, concerned. "Shoot anyone who comes through that door," he instructed.

"You can't go out there alone, Zur. Let me go with you," she pleaded.

"I won't hear it. You stay tight and protect this house." He roped his hand around his leather belt, slid the curved sheath of his knife loose, and showed Eleanora the blade. "I'll be back before you know it." He leaned in and kissed her on the head.

Maurel and Casey ditched the truck and ran into the subterranean entrance of the mine. The light died, forcing them to stay close and navigate the dirt walls by touch. They went far enough in then ducked behind a stack of crates, hoping to remain hidden long enough to catch a breath. Insulated by tons of earth, any movement or sound either of them made was amplified and would give away their position. Maurel whispered to Casey, grasping for a plan, but both fell silent when men with guns emerged behind brash echoes that stormed from the mouth of the mine. They had pulled up their truck as far as it would go and the blinding beams flooded the entrance. Outlines of the McShay gang approached in unison, their rifles drawn. Maurel grew sick as he realized that they were pinned down in their position with no direction to turn. To go back was almost certain death, but to head further underground without a light was to venture into oblivion. He peered over the edge of the crate, surprised to see the men had turned their backs and were now approaching someone else, who had ventured in after them.

"Who the hell is that?" Casey hissed. "I can't see a thing beyond those lights."

When the gang got close enough, they shined a lantern on the new intruder. Zuriel stood in his gray thermal underwear and boots, wielding his knife in the faces of the armed men. The boys recognized the hobbled shape as their father, and when a McShay raised a rifle, Maurel jumped from behind the crate and rushed him, knocking the gun to the ground. Casey went straight for Dunny McShay and cracked him in the face. Zuriel sliced up the man in front of him, but he and another man hugged Zuriel's arms to his sides and unloaded a series of crushing blows to his ribs and stomach. As the fight raged, Casey dropped to his knees and searched for the gun. He felt rock and sand and got his fingers caught under boot heels. A man fell over his back and thankfully took no notice of him. Casey could not produce the rifle. Instead, he unearthed the head of a pickaxe from out of the ground.

"Case!" yelled Maurel, dust shot through with bands of light. Casey popped up from the mirth below and threw the axe to his brother, who caught it firm and stared at it strangely, expecting to be clutching the gun, before he swung it high and hard at his attacker. The pick pierced through the brittle dome of bone at his temple and out the other side, fastening the dead man's head to the curved dirt celling above.

Familiar, holy visions coursed through Zuriel. He set his gaze
on his assailant, turned his shoulder to drawn him forth, exposing
his midsection, then came around low from the opposite side and
slid the full length of his blade in at the kidney. The tall body fell
over his shoulder and Zuriel flipped him over and crawled on top
of him. He wrapped his bicep around his throat, intertwined their
legs, and choked the man until the life coursed out of him.

The three Baynes struggled to their feet and made sure they
were not wounded. The boys brushed the dirt from their clothes
and came to realize that Dunny McShay was missing just as the
shadow of a rifle barrel extended through the caustic glare and
rested at the base of Zuriel's spine. The boys froze, their hands
out in front of them. Maurel was crouched down, and he lowered
one of his hands until he clutched hold of a jagged rock and raised
it up and smashed Dunny in the face before he could fire a shot.
He dropped his rifle and this time Casey recovered and righted the
gun. He handed it over. Maurel gritted his teeth and got out half
of the word motherfucker before firing three bullets in succession,
dropping Dunny in a heap.

The echo from the discharged rounds faded into a low vibra-
tion that grumbled throughout the surrounding earth. The low
ceiling began to leak hourglass streams of dirt between the rotted
trusses of wood. Maurel reached for his injured father, but Casey
grabbed his arm and held him back. The roof of the mineshaft
groaned and cracked as though it was being devoured by a great
machine. Their father collapsed on one knee, shielding himself
from falling dirt, when the main support buckled and the shaft
collapsed above Zuriel.

Casey pushed Maurel back toward the entrance and forced
him to run until their lungs tasted fresh open air. They sprinted
ahead of the collapse and dove beside McShay's truck, landing

on their chests. A torrent of rocks and dirt flew over their heads, swallowing the fallen McShays in the mouth of the mine and burying their father in the midnight of his tomb.

NINE

A PAIR OF GLOVED HANDS unearthed blue and tan fingerlings from neat mounds of dirt along the side of the Bayne house. Hulking pallid squash and enormous green beans swirled from the vines, which Jordan clipped and gathered in a bucket. Blueberries and blackberries fell from bushes, feverish and overgrown. He culled their fruit with a metal-toothed comb affixed to a coffee can. He hauled his varied bounty up to the kitchen and set it on the counter, where Walker was helping Elizabeth and her mother prepare jam pastries. Jordan wiped his neck with a rag and rummaged through his suitcase on the floor in the living room. Elizabeth stole a glance at his sweating back before he pulled a clean white shirt over his head. Jordan sensed her there and turned around, catching her off guard. "Would you like a drink?" she asked. "You look like you could use one."

Jordan nodded.

"I'll get you a beer," she said.

"Actually," Jordan stopped her. "I would like some of that lemonade, if you don't mind."

Elizabeth smiled. "Sure thing."

Malcolm came through the screen door misted with sweat himself, headphones still blaring from his morning run. Elizabeth kissed him and handed Jordan a cold glass of lemonade, then rejoined her mother in the kitchen. Jordan took the damp rag in his hand and threw it in his brother's face. He sneered, then used it to wipe his brow anyway.

Laughter erupted from the kitchen. The boys watched their father prance in an apron, flour on his nose and in his beard.

"What's got into him?" Malcolm pointed with the rag down the hall.

"The fairer of the Truitts, I imagine."

Mary was making the crust for her pie, folding chilled water and lard into the dough. "Don't feel bad," she taunted Walker. "No need to be ashamed of your rather pedestrian cooking."

Walker kneaded dough beside her on a wood block. "That's all right, ladies," he said. "I'd have you get your hands up rear of them ducks we're roasting tonight if I didn't think you'd have too good a time with it." He turned away as Mary and Elizabeth threw pinches of flour at him.

Jordan hovered over the pie fixings and stuck his finger in the fruit. Elizabeth slapped his hand away. "What's for dinner?" he asked.

"Main course is duck, roasted and stuffed. We're mashing those potatoes with fat from the bird, turn the collards in that, too. Cobbler of them brambles and, oh yes, a pecan pie."

"Sounds like we're fixing on a feast. Let me know if there's anything I can do to help."

Walker drew a slow laugh out of his belly, looking at both his sons. "Who y'all think's going to get us them ducks?"

Bethlehem Creek shimmered with incandescent waves that refracted the glare of the sun. Malcolm and Jordan suited up in rubber waders pulled from the trunk of Malcolm's SUV, each checking a pack of supplies and sight-lining their shotguns. On the narrow trail, their covered feet moved clumsy in the brush. They stumbled down the bank but managed to make it to the bottom of the slope that skirt-ed the contour of the shore. Slowly, their bodies submerged into the muck. Rings rippled in each direction and dispersed across the surface.

"I used to fish here," Malcolm said, disappeared up to his chest. He arched his neck, scanning the ash-colored sky for move-ment. They passed along the ridge of the shore, one behind the other. "Trout came easy here at the right time of year," he said. "Got a forty-inch muskie once."

"Bullshit," Jordan scoffed.

"All right, maybe that was Roscoe. He used to come down here to lay his girl, Marie." Malcolm could see Jordan smirking. "He told me about it, so what?"

"Nothing," Jordan said. "I didn't know you had friends in high school."

"Shut up."

After a few hundred yards the shelf dropped off, sending both of them sideways up to their chins. Elbows raised above the surface, they held their guns overhead. Eventually, they found their footing as the shallows rose to meet them. They followed a narrow slip that lead out to a raised finger of submerged grass that could not be accessed from any point on shore. Malcolm blew the duck call while Jordan cracked two cans of beer and handed one over, staying in place until the water grew still. The trees on shore hushed with the onset winds of autumn. Malcolm turned his ear to the bank across the gyre that churned in front of them.

"We used to do this all the time," Jordan said after the calm set.

"Man, what happened?" Malcolm took in fresh air and held it in his lungs.

"I don't remember much of nothing. Sometimes I think I have brain damage, I swear."

"No shock there," Malcolm said, sweeping his vision from side to side.

"How's that?" Jordan asked.

"Who knows what you know," said Malcolm. "I think back to when we were in school. You and I would drive around in your truck all summer, going to parties, fishing up at Beaver Lake. We would head down to New Orleans. Leave the city at dawn, fried out of our minds. We had some good times. I tried for years to figure out if something happened. You and I were okay, but by the time we finished school you just had the breath of hell in you. I didn't know where it came from. I was worried. Your friends said you were at the bar talking about leaving. Harrell said you blacked out and woke up in his truck, rambling about how everything was so fucked that you were either going to leave or kill yourself. He didn't think much of it, because, well, no offense, but we had all sort of gotten used to that kind of talk from you. So, I asked him what happened. He said he pulled over on the side of the road and you fell out the passenger side and threw up. After a minute he didn't hear nothing, so he went around the far side of the truck and you were gone, just like that."

A long-buried sorrow clawed its way through Jordan's chest and clenched shut the bottom of his throat. Malcolm looked over as his brother turned away. "I went off to college a couple months later. Had to move on, for better or worse."

"Sorry," Jordan muttered.

"Doesn't matter now," Malcolm told him. "We're standing up to our balls in muddy water, aren't we?"

Jordan angled his barrel across the sky, following a loon that flew a few hundred yards in a matter of seconds until it glided from sight. He lowered his shotgun.

Malcolm stuffed the crushed cans in his pack. He handed Jordan another beer. "We were talking the other day about music. Curious if you gave it any more thought."

"Who knows," said Jordan. "There are songs in my head I know I can write, I don't know why I don't."

"You could start by getting out of San Antonio. Go to Austin, or come back here. Stop fighting it."

"I think that's what I'm doing," Jordan admitted. "I like being back with you and Dad, and I'm happy you found someone."

Malcolm blew the high wheeze of the duck call and asked if Jordan had a girl, the question sprawling like a bridge to all he still didn't know about his life. "Saw you and Leah outside the bar the other night."

"She said she would consider seeing me again, to my amazement. Enough time must have passed to soften her entrenched desire to murder me."

Malcolm swished around in the water and aimed his rifle above Jordan's shoulder into a thick canopy of trees. A rustle rose from inside the wood. "Blow the call," Malcolm whispered.

A shrill note blew across the expanse—nothing. Jordan reached in the water and dug out a smooth black stone. He threw it in a long arc that landed with a hollow knock against the base of a tree, flushing three slender bodies from the brush. Jordan fumbled to aim and fired off a rogue shot that sent the birds flapping faster, gaining height. Malcolm took his time squinting down the track of his barrel, drew a sharp breath, and fired three steady shots. One duck continued to rise. The others faltered from the sky, landing with a hard splash in the shallow water.

Jordan spread a dead bird on the cutting block in the kitchen. The ligaments cracked at the base of the wings, but he wedged in the corrugated sheers and snapped through the muscle on each side. He made similar cuts on the rest of the ducks, then severed each set of bony legs above the joint. Two pots filled with water sat on the stove, steam pouring from one, the other cold. Jordan dropped a block of paraffin into the boiling pot, then gripped one of the carcasses by the neck and dunked it below the wax, coating the feathered body. He held each bird below the surface, pulled them out, and plunged them into the pot of cold water, solidifying the wax into a hard shell. He cracked open the wax with a knife and pried outward with his fingers, pulling the keratin quills out of the denuded skin in clusters. He worked the shoulders and breast until all the feathers were removed.

He severed their lifeless heads with a butcher's knife. Dark blood leaked out of each orifice and Jordan rushed to pinch them closed. He hooked his finger into the cavity at the neck and drew out the organ sack intact. More blood rushed across the table. He did the same to the other two, then scraped the vinous organs, severed heads, spiny feet, and bloody sinew into the trash.

"Look at those beauties," said Walker. He and Mary came into the kitchen carrying groceries. Jordan could tell the presence of women was making him lively and it was already wearing on his nerves. "Malcolm always was one hell of a shot," he continued.

Malcolm warmed himself up with a cup of tea. "What did I do?" he asked.

"Bagging these drakes for our feast," Mary said.

"Actually," Malcolm said, "Jordan nailed both of them."

He exchanged glances with his brother. Walker took a moment to stand corrected before patting Jordan on the shoulder as he passed, reticent to offer a knowing look of his own.

————

After dinner, those who were staying retreated to different corners of the house and Walker asked Jordan to join him in the garage. There was something he wanted to show him.

"An old friend sends me this tobacco he grows out in Virginia. If this ain't the best stuff you ever smelled," said Walker. He removed the lid from the crate to show Jordan huge brittle leaves stacked in parchment, sun-struck brown, sweetly aromatic. "I shred a couple at a time as needed, keep it in this jar for special occasions." Walker rolled two big cigarettes, fastening the single brown wrap over itself. He handed over a lighter and Jordan pulled his until it was lit and inhaled. They stood together, smoking in quiet.

"How come Uncle Jake ain't around no more? He was here all the time when we were kids, y'all were close." Walker glared through the purity of white smoke, not addressing the question, so instead Jordan asked him about Maurel. "I read the letters in his foot locker," he said. "I didn't know he was in the war."

Walker felt his face grow hot. "What's bringing this on, huh? For years you couldn't have been bothered to give a damn, now suddenly you're interested in family history?"

For once, Jordan decided to be honest with his father. "I've started to realize how little I know about us. There are gaps in my memory, things I can't remember happening or having done. I can't imagine what I've missed, and I mean all of it Mom, Jake, Grandpa Maurel. There's a lot I'm seeing for the first time. The more I find out, the more I want to know."

A disappointed sigh escaped Walker. "What's done is done. Let's work on getting the future right."

"See, that's exactly what I'm talking about," Jordan countered. "You didn't address anything I just said. Why does everything always have to be shrouded in such mystery?"

Walker sniped his smoke in the ashtray and smoothed down his beard. "Listen, boy," he said, solemn. "Believe me when I say, it ain't in some things' nature to be known."

Late that night, when the house was still, a low whisper crept over the arm of the couch as Jordan lay asleep. "Wake up," hissed Malcolm, jostling Jordan by the shoulder. "Come on, get up."

Jordan pried open his eyes to see Malcolm standing over him dressed in black, fiddling with two flashlights. "What are you wearing?" he asked, sitting up. Malcolm got one of the flashlights to work and turned it on inches from Jordan's face. He flung out his arm to defend against the blinding light. "I forgot how annoying you can be," he groaned.

"Let's go," Malcolm urged. "We're going out there."

Jordan mumbled, seduced by sleep.

"The grove in the woods," Malcolm said, hitting him again. "Remember?"

Jordan sat up and rubbed his eyes a final time. "It's two in the morning, and you want to go for a walk in the woods?"

Malcolm knew it was the sort of idea Jordan could never resist.

"We haven't been out there since we were kids. I wouldn't even remember how to get there," Jordan told him.

"I remember," said Malcolm. "Come on, follow me." He pulled the drawstrings on his hooded sweatshirt and tossed Jordan a black Carhartt jacket from the rack by the door. The flashlight bounced throughout the downstairs of the house as they escaped out the back.

Jordan followed Malcolm through thick brush at the end of the yard until they passed into the trees. The woods at night were interwoven with the fabric of silence. Malcolm looked at his watch with the flashlight, two minutes to three thirty in the morning. The waxing curve of the moon cast silver through a lattice of trees onto the earthen floor.

Malcolm spotted a familiar series of mounds and called for his brother to stop. Jordan circled back as Malcolm trained his light on a moldered, overgrown hill. "That's the entrance to the old mine," he said. "It was one of three entrances to the Legot system. The tunnels go all the way out to Harrison and Yellville."

"Think there's any way in?" he asked, circling the mound.

"It collapsed," said Malcolm.

They trekked on, timber hushed in twilight. Unknown to them, Cob concealed himself, keeping track of the brothers from behind a tree. They walked until the sky grew wide beyond the last stand of trees and opened onto an overgrown clearing. Jordan and Malcolm crossed into the expanse. With no tree cover, the field was far brighter than the forest, glowing in a mercurial haze. They came to a stop in the middle of the grove and Malcolm saw the bewilderment on his brother's face. They walked as far as the lone elm hung ancient over the edge of a small pond.

"I forgot this even existed," said Jordan. "Thank you."

Malcolm crouched at the water's edge, submerging his palm in the dark pool. "You and everyone else, apparently."

Jordan watched Malcolm wash his hand back and forth in the water.

"Did I ever tell you, I used to have this dream. Had it years ago when I was locked up, been having it again."

Malcolm stretched his vision into the dark as Jordan pointed toward the other end of the field.

"I come out of those trees over there. In front me there is this pervasive light, and shadows move across the stand of trees. Rows have been carved out of the vegetation and from the tree line I can see that they are connected to a maze of narrow pathways. I see a shadow move again, but this time I realize that it's not a shadow, it's a figure in a long black dress, harvesting the field. There are more of them, hunched over, their faces covered, using these big scythes to hack back the vegetation. Before I know it, I'm walking in the middle of the field and these women with the scythes begin to surround me. They shuffle up the rows single file with their scythes raised. I run back into the woods, trying to catch my breath."

Malcolm was rapt. "So, you get away?"

"I run all the way to the entrance of the mine, except it's not covered, it's wide open, so I go inside. The tunnel is pitch black, I walk with my hands out in front of me. The air grows cold, the shaft begins to descend. I'm scared that I've gone too far down the tunnel and I won't be able to find my way out, so I turn back. When I'm almost to the exit, I hear the women with the scythes coming toward me in the dark. I run back down the mineshaft and fall into a trench. I grab at the soil, but it pulls away in handfuls and I keep sliding. When I stop, I feel around and keep my hand against a dirt wall until it leads to the edge of a set of stairs. These stairs, they go down forever, and I descend into darkness without end."

Beneath the low-hanging boughs of the elm, Malcolm stared at their reflections wavering on the surface of the pond. "So, what happens then?"

"I wake up."

TEN

THE DIM SHAPES OF cars and trucks sulked through the early morning as Malcolm jogged past an auto body shop and dealer of hearths and sheds, both closed. Only the gas station on the corner flurried with workers for whom dawn was the norm.

He crossed into a wealthy neighborhood where big, nearly identical houses lined both sides of the street. A young woman loaded children into a Volvo wagon. A Rottweiler clawed the dirt along the worn pickets of a fence, his bark pleading for Malcolm's recognition. He sank in the solace of headphones, trotting through sprawling streets of homes with dozens of decorative rooms, vaulted atriums of glass, vibrant, manicured lawns, and the occasional pool glistening behind a private gate. Only the barely rich would cover entire houses in lavender and lime, neon monstrosities that protested the pallid pallet of an Ozark morning.

A gold SUV slowed beside Malcolm and lowered the passenger window. "Hey there, stranger." A dark-haired man craned to get a good look at Malcolm as they crept up the road. "Malcolm," he said. "It's Ben Ringgold."

Malcolm was slow to recognize his old boss. He removed his earbuds and leaned on the window.

"Sorry. Took me a minute," Malcolm said with an artificial inflection.

"Happens to me all the time," Ben said. "How the hell are you? Back in the old neighborhood, I see."

"So it seems. Actually, I'm getting married."

"Get out," he yelled. "Maybe I knew that. Martha handles the mail, she must have the invitation somewhere."

Malcolm stretched as he stood in place, bending back each of his legs at the knee. "Yeah, I don't know. I'm like you, that's Elizabeth's department."

"I live just up the hill. I'm sure you don't want to jog all that way," he said, popping the automatic lock. "What do you say? We'll get you some lemonade, a chance to catch up."

Morning glowed through the portico of the Ringgold house. Malcolm tracked in sand and pine needles on the heels of his running shoes, and no matter how lightly he stepped, his rubber soles squeaked on the polished tile. He sat on the soft gold couch at the center of a vast living room. Ben told him to make himself comfortable then hurried toward him in a panic, pushing Malcolm's back that was soaked with sweat, cautioning him not to lean against the delicate fabric. He went in the front room and returned with a bottle of Evian and a towel. Malcolm dried himself and sat forward in an awkward position.

The fat skin on Ringgold's cheeks turned an embarrassing red as though a secret of his had been exposed. Malcolm did his best to appear at ease, even though he sat bewildered by the bizarre occurrence of their chance meeting. Ringgold's incessant talking was interrupted by the television's constant flow and the echoing pangs of the big, bright room. He recounted the years since they had last seen each other and it became clear they had nothing in common besides the two years Malcolm worked for Ben out of high school. Malcolm was indifferent, but as they continued to talk, he was overcome by a subtle, creeping sense of shame, unable to escape the notion that this would be his life in the not-too-distant future. Without ever noticing, Malcolm's life had gradually grown devoid of any activity not centered on money. All his time and interests were accounted for and he had not considered how nominal and one-dimensional any of it was until he came face to face with the ephemera of his future prison. He did not like what he saw.

The door from the garage cracked shut and Ben's wife came in with two armfuls of bags. Dyed blonde hair pulled back, she scampered in pink yoga pants across the tiled floor onto the carpet in the living room. Her bony frame slid in loose-fitting skin.

"Ben, dear," she crowed. "You didn't tell me we had a guest."

"He's derelict, honey. I picked him up off the street." Ben winked. "Please, take pity on the boy."

Malcolm put out his hand and Martha Ringgold examined him with a sidelong stare.

"If it's not little Malcolm Bayne," she exclaimed. "My God, sugar, look at you all grown up." She stepped back before rushing up and pressing her chest against him.

The phone rang and Ben stepped out to take the call in his home office, sliding the oak door closed behind him. Martha returned from the kitchen with two fogged glasses of Myers's and lemonade. She handed Malcolm his and let her manicured fingers fall inside his thigh. She grazed her hand in a small circle and pursed her waxy lips. "You were just the freshest little thing when you worked for us all them years ago. I wanted so bad to taste that juice when it was still young and sweet. Suppose you think that's silly."

"You know I am back here to get married," he said.

"Who cares about a thing like that? I'll let you in on a little secret," she whispered. "It just makes it even better."

Martha's eyes went white with pleasure. She took the contour of Malcolm's crotch in her grip. Malcolm tossed her hand aside and shot to his feet, flustered. Beneath her illicit, ill-timed advance lurked a deep loneliness that pulled anything it could toward it. A sickness hit Malcolm like an aftershock. This chance visit with his old boss and his wife was on the verge of disgrace, catalyzing in the one sip of lemonade and rum burning at the top of Malcolm's stomach. He found his coat in the foyer and flew out the front door.

Jordan's truck cut through traffic until buildings and cars lessened between mile markers and swatches of pine on the way to Mountain Home, where his Uncle Jacob lived, twenty minutes outside of town. He made a right onto a dirt road that snaked midway up a bluff. As he watched the numbers on rusted mailboxes tick upward, the subtle gnaw of nervousness crept over him. He had worked it over in his head the whole drive and was worried Jake would refuse to speak to him, suspecting an ulterior motive. What was there to say to an uncle he had not seen for half his life?

Tires snapped to a stop on the gravel in front of a small white house with blue shutters. Jordan killed the engine and stared at the front door, almost not realizing he had arrived until he saw Jacob slumped in the narrow doorway.

He stood taller than Walker, his black hair combed back, falling behind one ear. His heavy eyes and grim mouth consternated at the sight of the unexpected visitor as he hoofed down the concrete steps and stood in front of the truck. Jacob relaxed his posture when he recognized Jordan. He went back inside and Jordan followed.

"Wouldn't mind skippin' the niceties, if it's all the same to you," Jacob said.

Jordan sat in a chair and let out some nervous air, afraid the opportunity to talk was already dwindling. "I suppose you are wondering why—"

"Why you're sinking into my leather?" Jacob cut him off. "As a matter of fact, I am a bit curious."

"I been gone a while, Jake, and I ain't seen you in twice as long. I came home for Malcolm's wedding," Jordan said.

"Your brother's getting married?" he asked. "The time does go."

Jordan agreed. "Anyway, I've been noticing things, learning about our family. There is a lot I was never aware of, and, you know, I been thinking—"

"Get on with it," Jacob insisted.

"Why don't you and my father talk anymore?"

Jake snickered and sat up straight on the edge of his chair, rubbing the flats of his palms together, gathering a notion. "He never told you?"

Jordan shook his head.

"Maybe you should ask him, then. Last I want to do is dig up what's long been dead."

The massive head of a trophy buck jutted from the wall behind Jacob, its face still frozen between the terror of Jacob's bullet and the resignation of death.

"We were hunting," Jacob started. "Me, your dad, and your grandfather, Maurel. We were in a valley on the southeastern edge of the Boston Mountains. I hit one the first night, we dressed her there in the field and and then threw her on the fire for dinner. We was all sipping off rye—that was your grandpa's drink. He was first to turn in. I tamped the fire and remember your father talking about the constellation Orion. That's you, he told me, the hunter. I went off to sleep while your father gathered garbage from around the campsite and stored it in a sack with the trimmings from the deer.

Next I know, our father's screaming in his tent. When I got to him, the tent was torn to shreds. I crawled inside and found him soaking in a bag of his own blood. He had been mauled by a brown bear. Your dad ran up, panicked. We cleaned Maurel's wounds with whiskey and river water, then bandaged him up. He had lost so much blood and we were hours from a hospital. I fashioned a gurney from one of the tents and we carried him on it a few miles until we got back to my truck. Before we left, I saw the bag of garbage ripped open back at the site. Your dad left it out. That's what drew the bear into our camp." Jacob bared his teeth, blinking as though there was something wrong with his eyes. "I was furious. We drove for over an hour before dad started to seize. There was nothing to be done, so Walker climbed into the back seat and put him out of his misery. We brought his body back to your house," he said coldly.

"We tried for a while after to pretend that none of it happened the way it did, but I couldn't even look him in the eye. Pa's death opened an abyss between us that neither of us could face, so we went our separate ways. No matter how much your father apologized, no matter what remorse or recompense he gave, I just thought it would never be enough, considering what he had taken from me." Jacob fell silent, considering his words before he continued on. "I am a man of faith, Jordan, so I am confident a man such as Maurel Bayne got to where he was supposed to be going. There are some things, though, that cannot be forgiven, no matter how hard we try. Pray to God you never find out what they are."

Jordan used to play music in Springfield, just over the Missouri border. It was a small college city with a rich musical history. He had played a lot of the bars in town, but his favorite was a spot called Tim's, and that's exactly where he was headed. He called Leah on the drive, but she didn't pick up. So he called Georgia, an ex-girlfriend from Springfield, who agreed to meet him at Tim's at eight o'clock that night.

Georgia was a small, fiery brunette. In the years Jordan had seen her, they proved to be exceedingly dangerous for each other, a match tossed in a pool of gasoline. When they drank to excess, which was always, they laid a trail of wreckage from bar to bar that followed the same pattern of beer, whiskey, weed, and pills, landing them in a cheap motel room. Then the real drinking began, the kind functioning human beings don't know exists, solely the trade of the violent, depressed, and insane. A hatch would open inside of Jordan and a black hose would snake straight out of his gut, ravenous for something to drink, someone to hate, ready to devour. This went on for years, undisturbed.

Jordan had thrown Georgia out with the bathwater, while she went on her own way. Now they sat across from each other, watching people stroll past the window at Tim's. Vodka softened Georgia's voice as she filled Jordan in about an abusive boyfriend and their disastrous move to Orlando. That stretch of misery lasted for two irrevocable years before she split in the forty-eight hours that Salvador, that was his name, sat in lockup for hocking hydrocodone to despondent teenagers and dopesick mothers. She moved back to Springfield and began bartending, a gig she didn't mind so much compared to the horror show that was her life in Florida. She said the Ozarks were easy to leave and even easier to come back to, which Jordan seconded. When Georgia's mother died, she got the house. "The only gift she ever gave me," she said, rolling her midnight eyes.

"Except life," Jordan said. "She did give you that."

"Oh, beautiful boy," she said. "How I missed you."

On the cab ride back to her house, Georgia put her thick cotton lips on Jordan's and they enveloped each other with unthinking force. She pulled a bottle from the bottom cabinet in her kitchen, poured a bourbon over ice and handed it to him, then knelt and undid his belt. Georgia searched for Jordan's hands, which she drew up behind her ruminating head. She interlocked her fingers with his, then shoved her mouth down on his length. His bones shattered with relief. He continued with the force she had introduced and grabbed her by a handful of hair and led her to the couch. Georgia knelt on all fours and pushed her eyes closed in the cushions. Jordan tore his shirt from overhead and saw himself, an opaque animal reflected in the window, where he watched Georgia's eyes go blank and mouth contort as he spread her flesh to each side and slid.

He woke later, tangled in skin and blankets, too late to return home and far too late to meet Leah, if she'd come after all. He kept going over the story Jacob had told him about the bear. There was something essential that he felt he was approaching, but it was still so far away. The truth had been broken into so many pieces that no single picture might ever emerge. Jordan got up and splashed more whiskey in his watered glass, then stood at the window, watching the lights of the city glow in twilit slumber.

ELEVEN

The devout congregation of Divine Light Ministries heaved a tent pole under a flapping canvas that they cranked into place and roped to the ground. The men and their sons wore straw hats and rolled their striped sleeves while women of every age focused on the sanctimony of their task with uniformly grim consternation, their flowery dresses billowed by the wind.

Not long after he crossed the dried river delta and caught the ferryboat to Mississippi, Zuriel Bayne witnessed the transmutation of divine spirits and the rapture of human bodies pulled straight into the air and back down again by a cause none other than the holy word of God. From then on his mind, body, and soul burned with the fire of Pentecost. Zuriel left sharecropping the family farm and dedicated his efforts to the revival of Charles Parham, a dashing dark-haired preacher who had made a name for himself on the backs of snakes and song. Zuriel joined other followers who, like him, had left all they knew in order to spread the Word wherever it could be heard, mostly in the empty lots and railroad stops of southern towns.

Zuriel's wife Eleanora began receiving grainy postcards of their tent staked in some rural field, the notes on the back written in her husband's telling scrawl. Zuriel missed her something

awful, lying on his cot finished with the day's work, only scripture, he told her, able to rid him of the lovesick pain that speared
his heart. Even the good book did not always work as intended.
As time wore on, elaborate letters replaced those forlorn notes
and any mention of her was relegated to *Eleanora, you must witness
the spectacle I have helped to create,* or, *These people are sick and their
contagion is fear. They are plagued by nothing more than their own imper-
manence! How do they not see that they live forever in Christ? Demons have
their sights set on the righteous. Many have already earned their way into
the purest of hearts.* He disparaged every aspect of modern life in
long, unbroken tracts—lust and vice, drink, tobacco, false idols,
and religions. He sent one letter that was entirely about electric-
ity. *We are opening ourselves up to attack,* he warned her. *They are coming through the wires.* The irrational turned irate, his anger devolved
to hatred. Eleanora watched as the same inert force that caused
the fragile to go insane consumed her husband until she dropped
his last letter in disgust, unable to recognize the man who was
speaking.

When he did come home for two weeks, his main concern
was arranging her a proper baptism in the creek. Eleanora didn't
mind, she was a woman of belief and modest conviction and rel-
ished what diligence she could offer the Lord in her own way. But
in her heart, she mourned the loss of Zuriel. After he up and left
again, he resumed the same veiled incertitude, and eventually his
letters made no mention of her at all. She bundled the letters and
deposited them in the top drawer of her bureau, adding each new
one to the pile unread.

The house sweltered in June. Eleanora had done her part with the
rest of the family to take care of Sherman, Zuriel's ailing father.
His fever had turned rheumatic and the chronic coughing and fits

of delirium were getting worse. She sent for Zuriel, who returned from south Texas four days later by train.

When Zuriel stepped into his father's room, the shades were drawn. Even though it was cool and dimly lit, the air was choked by a foul humidity, the sort that only comes with sickness. Its stench wafted down the hall, reminding Zuriel of the tuberculosis wards he had visited in his travels, scores of crippled convalescents packed together like sardines. His eyes watered and throat cinched as much from his father's body fighting the scourge of influenza as the waves of dread rushing forth, a son's fear of seeing his father incapacitated, a reminder of frailty that made loving a painful risk and the duty of hating him that much more difficult.

"I came as soon as I heard," he told Eleanora, who tended to his father. His brother Jonathan kneeled at the bedside. "How is he holding up?"

"Each day worse than the last, I reckon." Eleanora leaned across Sherman to fix his sheet and turn the washcloth on his forehead to the side that was fresh and cold, careful not to wake him.

Zuriel recited scripture to himself, *As a father has compassion on his children, so the Lord has compassion on those who fear him; for he knows how we are formed, he remembers that we are dust.* When his brother glared at him, he stopped, repeating the line another twelve times in his mind, as well as another psalm that said, *All our days pass away under your wrath; we finish our years with a moan. We finish our years with a moan, we finish our years with a moan.* He gathered the courage to counter Jonathan's solemn stare.

"Nice of you to show up," Jonathan said.

"It was four days from San Antone, I left as soon as I got word."

"Out there saving everybody who needs it while your own father's six feet from dying back home."

"You got that wrong, John," said Zuriel.

"You'll have to explain it to me later, then."

The sour stench of salt hung on his shoulders. He had not felt more vulnerable or lowdown woeful than he did right then, so he resolved, for the sake of those involved, to stay out of the way. They watched Sherman sleep, his dry lips cracked open, talking through a dream. A slow breath decompressed his big chest, which pumped up again then fell beneath the blankets.

"How did you manage to get him to sleep?" Zuriel asked.

"Codeine." Jonathan grabbed the tincture from the nightstand and shook it in the air. "Want some?"

Zuriel slid his tall body through the doorway and stormed to the opposite corner of the house, cursing his brother. He drank from a cold bottle of milk he pulled from the icebox. Once he calmed down, he realized how tired he was. The revival was never short on tasks to be done. He had been working tirelessly with his brethren each day without so much as a break. Even the train ride home was arduous—boxcars smashing headlong down the rails, children crying, passengers gossiping, complaining about the heat that trapped them all in its noxious cloud. Maybe returning home was a blessing after all. Before he knew it, despite the taunts of his brother, Zuriel fell to sleep on top of the made guest bed, his cracked leather shoes kicked to the floor. Eleanora found him there, hat lowered over his eyes, shielding him from the world. She turned out the lamp and closed the door behind her, leaving him to sleep for two days straight.

Three weeks later, Sherman's condition had improved. Eleanora got him to melt an ice cube on his tongue as she read stories from the newspaper. He grew more responsive each day, sitting up on a stack of pillows, reading the paper, Chaucer, the Bible, soaking up the light that came through the window, even singing hymns with

Eleanora. He held down chicken broth and drank tea with hibiscus honey to maintain his blood sugar. After two months in bed, he stretched both legs and finally planted his paper-thin feet on the wood floor. He made it down the stairs a few days later without informing anyone and sat in the rocker in the front room, petting their Persian Blue. Eleanora, Zuriel, and Jonathan could not believe what they were witnessing and rejoiced.

Unknown to everyone else, it was during this time that Zuriel began hearing his own voice fracture and echo back to him, distorted. He had grown forgetful, but never more stubborn, insisting on versions of events that had never happened. He stopped sleeping. Ceaseless chatter could be heard throughout the house at any hour of the night. Eleanora dragged around her skinny frame, worried sick about Zuriel, left with no way to approach him that did not result in some hysterical episode. Half moons hung swollen below her eyes, her face ghastly and frail. She begged Zuriel to eat. He agreed but would only eat the Libby's corned beef that came in cans. Mam' Bayne kept them stocked in the pantry aside jarred gizzards and preserves. Eleanora couldn't keep a bite down herself. She would occasionally spread some cream butter on a cracker and get what delight from it she could. She stuck to her tea and drank it in places of refuge in the house where she found solace, leaving her husband alone in a world only he seemed to occupy.

The doctor visited for his last checkup. Sherman had improved remarkably but still coughed in spells, moved slow, and often fell because of swells of grave weakness that forced him to walk with a cane. The doctor suggested a routine Thorazine shot might serve to rebalance his equilibrium and elucidate his tension.

They gathered at the base of the stairs discussing their father's condition when, for no reason, Zuriel snapped. He lunged toward Doctor Gustavson and closed his hands around his throat. "May

Saint James strike the poisonous pageantry from your hand!" he yelled. The doctor shielded himself from Zuriel's attack and somehow kept him from prying his medical bag from his grip until Jonathan forced them apart. Eleanora cried out and ran to Doctor Gustavson's aid. He smoothed his strands of blond hair and straightened his bifocals. Jonathan charged his brother backward until he had him cornered in the kitchen.

"What in God's name has gotten into you?" Jonathan yelled.

"That is precisely what has gotten into me, the holy word of our loving Christ!" Zuriel continued to pace back and forth, but Jonathan wouldn't let him through.

"Spare me the Christ fervor, you lunatic. Hey, look at me." Jonathan pulled Zuriel close and repeated the question. "Why did you choke the doctor?"

"He comes in this house, first he pumps Pa up with codeine, Pa's got a bit of trouble walking—he's old!—and this viper's ready to prick his arm with a Thorazine needle!" Zuriel raised his voice to make sure the doctor heard. "Look at him, clutching his bag of devilish tricks. Rotten peddler. Believe his day is coming, Jonathan. Yes sir, the holy spirit gone force a reckoning so this man poisons and deceives no longer!"

Jonathan and Eleanora were swathed with embarrassment and apologized ceaselessly as they helped the doctor to the door. A line had certainly been crossed, but none of them knew just how far Zuriel would go.

A month before Zuriel returned home and began his slide into madness, the Grand Lodge of the Free and Accepted Scottish Rite of Freemasonry awarded Jonathan Bayne his medal of initiation into their twenty-fifth degree, crowning him a Knight of the Brazen Serpent.

Though he belonged to the local in Carrollton, he traveled to the Grand Lodge in Little Rock for the ceremony. There he relinquished the various symbols and medals he held as Prince of the Tabernacle, then the elders cloaked him in a velvet robe and adorned him with a jeweled scepter as they read the rites of his new oath. One of the proudest moments of his life and he was there alone. Of course, that was the way all must arrive on the path of spiritual development. But he could not ignore that, save his lodge brothers, and the larger brethren of the Little Rock temple whom he barely knew, he had no loved ones or family there to share his achievement, no one to congratulate him once the ritual was complete.

Crickets threw their symphony into a night Jonathan took in on the porch. He too was worried about Zuriel and contemplated heavily the nature of his affliction. He applied specific rites and individual lessons that the Mysteries had taught him in order to find a way to help his brother. Benevolence toward others who were suffering and an unwavering dedication to truth were paramount ideals to the true Mason, and because the subject Jonathan was concerned with was his own brother, he weighed the severity of the problem even more so. The death of the soul was of great concern, but for his brother to perish was unthinkable.

When Jonathan thought of his brother, though, a towering wall of pity and anger arose. He could not help Zuriel if he still passed judgment upon him, and how could he judge Zuriel when he had not yet examined his own feelings and attitudes toward him? He struggled to move past the diversion of his anger and concentrate on the sadness that followed and threatened to consume his brother. He believed the evangelist's need to save and be saved was born of selfish desperation. Furthermore, to have this vain effort acknowledged not by fellow men or an officer of the

Church but by Christ himself, that was the most insane expectation of all. He hated Zuriel for insisting on the necessity of salvation for every living soul, that other people needed be saved and that he was the one to do it. He distrusted the surety of a belief like that because it was not open to him or the world. If anything, it showed disdain for the world by wanting so badly to leave it.

Jonathan actualized this through the pain of his reflection. My brother desperately wants to die, he thought to himself. How could he hate Zuriel for that? He wished he could comfort him, tell him how we survive our own funerals and live on past death, that we return to eternal creation anew. Through Christ or the void, it didn't matter. Zuriel would need to make that change within himself before he could reasonably expect the world to respond to the demands of his character or his beliefs. As he pressed on, Jonathan grew more frustrated. No, he said aloud, feeling himself getting closer to the root of the problem. That was a mere discrepancy of logic. He felt something essential rise in him and began to cry. If I could say only one thing to him, what would I say? he pondered. Jonathan's mind cleared as he came upon the answer—you do not need to die to be able to accept love.

He needed to find his brother and tell him how he felt. He leapt from his seat on the porch and paced through the house until he popped his head out the back door. He found Eleanora and Sherman fast asleep in their bed, but Zuriel was gone.

The five-cent rooms at Baker's Saloon were occupied by rough-shod drunks who slept off benders and opium eaters who climbed the tethers of hellish bliss in a slow-unfolding silence only broken by the whores screaming in the toilet at the end of the hall as they struggled to piss through the ravages of syphilis. They avoided and laughed at the mad Christian who shouted repentances through the door of room three each time they shuffled past.

Zuriel had no idea how long he had been there, but it was long enough for him to be caught in the ecstatic peaks and horrific depths of a revelation. Snakes worked through the woodwork as the whores of Babylon hurled their taunts. Zuriel stood poised on the bed, sermonizing to the wall. "Hard to believe I didn't see it earlier, hard to believe my own flesh and blood, an adept of the occult. How could my brother, my own likeness, not see that in a world of light and dark he has stood opposite me? Perturber, blasphemer of God's holy creation! He toys with nature and tears at the very fabric drawn across the wellsprings of Hell that serve to keep our demons imprisoned. Touting reason and self-analysis as the foundation from which you master your own soul, he taunts the echelons of angels and the entire divine order of heaven! Poor fool, duped by jinn, prostrate to the illusions of warlocks! Reason *is* faith, brother! True knowledge is not knowing! These idols of yours, these high priests of Egypt, mystagogues of Aryavarta, Kabbalistic Christ killers, they have all been dispelled by the glory of the true Redeemer! Dethroned by the empire of our cosmic Christ!

"No wonder our father fell ill in my absence. There is a plague in his house and his name is Jonathan. I was brought back to face this demon festering inside him that controls his every move. The life is being drained from this family, and soon there will be none of us left. No one is prepared to do what is required." He looked around him as bolts of lightning struck snake carcasses from the floor. "This room is protected by light," he announced. "Shown the paladin's way, armed with a sword of light, I am pure! I am blessed!" Zuriel knelt, holding his hands together. "Dear God, hear this prayer and accept it as my promise—I will save Sherman Bayne, beloved father, patriarch, sovereign of the Lord. I will draw forth any foe that seeks to do this family harm and will face it no matter how monstrous or familiar. Face the enemy, vanquish the darkness within. I swear this to you, amen."

Hours passed stretched by tremors before a loud knock woke Zuriel on the floor. His constitution was poor, his muscles twitched from malnutrition. He was subsisting in a state of constant animalic fear. Beleaguered, he hid behind the far side of the bed as the knocking continued.

Sherman held himself up with a cherrywood cane, conversing with Jonathan about the best way to get Zuriel to open the door. They had a plan to get him to a hospital in Hot Springs, where he would receive proper care. They only needed Zuriel to let them into the room.

"You in there, Zur? It's your brother, open up."

Zuriel rose from his knees and searched his clothes in the top drawer of the dresser until he produced a Savage .32. He gripped the machined steel and paced the floor.

"Come on, I can hear you in there. Please, open the door," Jonathan reiterated.

"You ain't my brother!" Zuriel shouted through the wood. "You use his voice, Ifrit." He laughed. "I'm sure you even present yourself similar, but I know the demon's penchant is to deceive. Underneath our common likeness you're hiding horns and eyes redder than a harvest sunset."

"I maintain to you, Zuriel, that I don't look like no devil, a truth you could easily ascertain if you opened the damn door." Jonathan cocked his ear and saw Sherman wince at his side. "What?" he asked his father.

"Nothing," Sherman elaborated. "Just, that is something a demon would say." Sherman's voice was tender from months of sick. He coughed and gripped the wall.

"What's that noise?" Zuriel asked. "Who's that with you, Jon? The law?"

"No police," Jonathan assured him.

Sherman got it together and stepped up to the door. "Zuriel, this is your father. I want to know that you're all right. How about you let us in? No one out here is going to hurt you, son, I promise."

"Ho, if that ain't a fine impression!" Zuriel smashed the gun against the door, repeating the word *no, no, no* as he drove his skull into the wood until his forehead was caked with blood. In his mind, he saw a creature with gray skin, sharp teeth, and long nails trying on members of his family like costumes. It was the same demon he had seen ever since he was a child. He had been watching it appear for weeks now, transforming into his brother, telling him lies in his voice, like there wasn't no law waiting to drag him off to prison, and that his Pa was out there beside him in that hall, healthy as can be, when he knew that old Sherman Bayne could not hobble more than a cursed yard to save his life.

Jonathan attempted to find some middle ground with his brother. His voice carried down the hallway. "Evil is temporary in this life. You know as well as I that good is the only force strong enough to prove eternal." He recalled the tenets of his Masonic teachings, hoping to find an aspect of his illumination that would also apply to the beliefs Zuriel held so dear. "The soul begs to return to its source in heaven, but in order to do that it must grow and suffer in the body. That is what we all must do, together."

Zuriel held the gun flat against his temple, driving it into his hair and sliding the metal against a crimson streak of blood. Then he raised his voice and called out a reply. "In the battle for my soul, I have been sanctioned as a holy apostle to stand against the wicked. The fight has brought me here, to this battlefield, where the lives of loved ones are won and lost. Satan sent a devil to infiltrate my life. He turned my brother to sorcery and used that portent to sicken my father. I see now that the battle was for my soul all along." Zuriel's face went slack with wonder. "To keep me from gaining my station in the kingdom of the Lord," he said, refreshed. "I am emboldened by my faith, scourged of fear, immune to the illusions of idols and persuaders of every kind." Zuriel ran to the opposing wall of the room then back, within arm's length of the door, where he spread his feet wide and squared his shoulders. "I call you forth, minion of hell. Emerge from where you are hidden so that you may be judged!"

Sherman held himself up by his cane on the other side of the door as it exploded with eight nickel-sized holes. Bullets splintered the wood and hit whatever was in their path with fury. When the shooting stopped, Jonathan uncovered his face to find his father heaped in blood, gasping for breath on the floor. The door hung shredded on its hinges. Jonathan pushed it open the rest of the way to find Zuriel, pistol smoking, casings scattered at his feet, grinning at the righteousness of his apocalyptic deed.

TWELVE

ELIZABETH DREW BACK THE opaque curtains that dressed the windows in the living room and watched the caterers in white collared shirts carry banquet tables and wheel out racks of chairs for the rehearsal dinner. Her attention drifted to a grainy picture of Malcolm and Jordan's mother, Mercy, framed in gold on the mantle. She thought it must have been from the late seventies. Her plain brown hair was parted evenly to each side, her milky complexion poured aside wide lavish eyes.

Walker startled her. "Thinkin' on Mercy?" he asked.

"She was beautiful," Elizabeth said, clutching the cheap frame.

"Loving that woman treated me to graces I thought a world like this could never offer," said Walker. "The beautiful are dealt a particular sort of cruelty. No worse than anybody else, of course. Just different." Walker's voice caught brittle in his throat. "The world she gave me, it was enough for a lifetime. I don't need to love again."

"Malcolm doesn't talk about her much," she told him. "They grew up without her?"

Walker brushed her aside to stand in the perennial light of the window. "She succumbed to uterine cancer four years after she had the boys. They had just begun to grow into the people they would become. Neither Mercy nor I saw it coming, how it set so fast. She wadn't ever lively about much, but she was sturdy as oak and almost never sick."

Elizabeth listened intently, framed by the window, holding the top button of her blouse.

"You know everything that happens with cancer? Tired all the time, cramping won't quit, can't eat nothing. It all happened in the span of two months." His voice broke, he covered the scruff of his mouth. "We were headed into winter, thought maybe she had a virus. Her color went. That's when I knew it was more. That Thanksgiving me and the boys took turns feeding her stuffing and pudding at the hospital. The only way I'd leave that room was to get flowers and the paper. I pulled a new white rose from a bouquet someone had sent and held it under her nose each morning. Waking her became harder to do. Pretty soon all she did was sleep, and so I slept on the floor beside her bed.

"Her family came from Fort Smith, we never got on. Her father hated Catholics more than Jews but not as much as blacks, and her mother blamed Mercy for every ill that befell them since she shat her out in that Depression-era shack and left her for dead. I told her she finally got what she wanted. They said their goodbyes, I wouldn't bring the boys in until they left. Folded back the sheet, sat them in her arms." Walker let Mercy's last moments wash over him. "Never saw her so serene as she was then. In that moment, I saw all that was supposed to be, this life of ours, what I thought the future might have been. I had a vision, that the boys were older, with wives and kids of their own running around this old place. Mercy was older still, tears of joy like jewels, proud of what we created. She died in her sleep the next morning."

Elizabeth nestled her head on Walker's shoulder and together they watched the caterers walk back and forth in front of the window.

Malcolm led a train of people up the back steps. Harrell, Russ, Baron, Johnny the bartender, and Josh Bodine, the bass player from Jordan's first band, procured bottles from the fridge and crowded around the island in the kitchen. Malcolm walked past Russ as though he didn't exist. He was only there because Harrell begged Jordan to let him come. Malcolm called for Elizabeth and found her standing with Walker. She shook her solace and asked about all the excitement.

"That would be the lineup of scholars Jordan put together for my bachelor party," he joked.

"He told me not to say anything," she admitted. "He was working real hard these last few days to pull it together."

"An impressive last-minute effort, as always."

Elizabeth rubbed his arm. "You're going to have so much fun."

"Where's he got off to?" Malcolm said, looking around the living room. He glanced at his father.

"Don't look at me," said Walker. "I ain't seen him since yesterday."

"What do you mean you haven't seen him?" Malcolm asked.

He went out to the hall and asked the guys in the kitchen if any of them had talked to his brother. None of them had. "He just told us to show up here," Baron explained. "We figured he was with you."

"Then what the hell are we doing here?" Malcolm threw up his arms and paced beside Elizabeth.

The guys had already been putting down beers at an industrial rate and were starting to grow restless. After a few attempts, Russ managed to get Jordan on the phone. "I got him," he told Malcolm. "He's in Springfield."

"Taking his sweet ass time getting back here?" Malcolm asked.

"Sounds like he's on a pretty good drunk." Russ downed his beer. "Says he can't drive."

Malcolm clenched his eyes and Elizabeth rubbed his shoulder. "All right," he said abruptly. "Get your shit, we're going to Springfield."

The Chop House was famed for serving sides of cow larger than blown tires in a setting of catalog décor and fake candlelight. Wine was poured and orders were placed, and since most of the bachelor party was made up of Jordan's friends, not Malcolm's, conversation was painful at first. Jordan faded in the far seat of the booth. Baron took responsibility for rousing him back to life by feeding him some aspirin that Jordan chewed instead of swallowed, and the guys all watched as the blue dust fell from his tongue. He folded his forearms on the table and planted his head.

Baron nudged him awake, waving a wine glass below his nose. "Hey, pal, drink this. Right bank Bordeaux, the good shit."

Jordan slurred softly. "When did you get into wine, big shot?"

"Shit, I'm cultured." Baron took a sip, feigning the learned reflection of a sommelier. "Remember my brother Derek? Yeah, he's queer now. Works for a wine distributor in Sonoma, ships a case home every Christmas."

Jordan raised an eye above the table, grabbing the glass and somehow drinking from it. "Derek's gay?" he asked.

Baron nodded.

"Good for him," said Jordan.

Enlivened by an unseen force, Jordan swung his glass to the center of the table, spilling a trail of wine across the white cloth. "I want to toast my brother," he announced, forehead still planted flat on the table. "We may not have been the closest brothers these past few years, but that is my fault. I think a lot of things are my fault because I done a lot of bad shit."

"You don't have to do this," Malcolm whispered.

He smacked his tongue against his teeth and sipped his wine before continuing on. "I'm not doing anything. I'm saying for the first time that I am trying to do something. Something good, you know? To be good, I guess. To be good to myself. To you, Dad, Elizabeth." He hiccupped. "I like your bride, Mal. She radiates pure goodness. I don't want her to hate me. I want you guys to call me on a day like a Tuesday and say hey, we were talking, and we want you to come down to Little Rock for the weekend. Stay with us, it's no problem." He maintained a grandiose gesture with his raised arm.

"There's a lot I don't say, but I will. I have a lot more to give. You know, I see everything? I am a watcher, so says the gypsy in Marfa. Observing is my role, she told me. Suffer is what I do." He clutched his shirt, shaking loose a phantom. "You are the doer, that's your role. All you ever do turns to gold. I followed your every step because you just knew. You knew when I shouldn't have jumped my bike, when cops were going to crash the party, when rain was coming hours before any signs of a storm. You got one killer instinct. How did you do that?" he asked. "Everything is so inherent with you. That is why you and Elizabeth, it's going to be good, you'll know what to do." He raised a stained glass, his hand covered in wine. "To us miserable fucks, to goodness, and truth. To you." Jordan toasted his brother, and the low voices of the men adhered.

"What was the original plan before we had to come up here and grab this degenerate?" Malcolm asked the group.

"We were supposed to go to New Orleans, stay in the French Quarter, hit a strip club, end the night at a riverboat casino," Harrell explained. "Sorry, man."

"I have to say, that sounds like it would have been so much more fun," he joked.

Jordan shoved him ahead on the bricks.

"All is not lost. We just have to find a place we can gamble." Malcolm was attempting to level with Jordan but he had slowed behind and stood at the curb, staring at a building across the street. Malcolm paced back to his brother. "Hey, I was just fucking with you," he said.

Jordan pulled a silver case from his jacket, lighting one of the cigarettes Walker had given him. Baron's low voice hollered after him and they all walked back up the sidewalk to where he stood. Jordan pointed across the street, smoke between his fingers. "That there's the Little Theatre, used to be the Landers Theatre. Tons of people played there. Flatt and Scruggs, June Carter, Roy Acuff, Red Foley, Pee Wee King." He stopped. "Come on," Jordan groaned. "Speedy Haworth, Tex Morton, fucking *Les Paul?*"

Russ shrugged in his jacket, Baron did little to hide his look of unknowing. "I heard of Les Paul," said Harrell. "He's the guy that makes the guitars."

Josh Bodine keeled over, laughing. Jordan looked at the lot of them. "You should be ashamed of yourselves," he said. He jogged across the street after a passing car and disappeared into the alley beside the theater. By the time they filtered into the alley after him, Jordan had gotten a foothold on the bottom rung of the fire escape, the whole iron apparatus clanking under his weight.

Malcolm peered up through the grate. "What are you doing up there, exactly?"

"Finding a way in," he answered, the orange pin of his cigarette glowing above their heads. Josh sprinted ahead and caught the lowest corrugated rung. He took the same route and joined Jordan on the walk.

"This is great and everything, but I would rather not have tonight end in breaking and entering and a trip to the Springfield jail. I do have to get married Saturday." Malcolm knew his brother could not hear him, so he went back to the street and looked both ways, casually accepting his role as spotter in a felony. "Selfish son of a bitch," he seethed to himself.

Five minutes later, Josh came down the mounted rungs and peeked over the side. "He's in," he whispered.

Malcolm was last to climb through the tall window that let out in the men's bathroom on the second-floor gallery. The group had already split up and Malcolm followed the red velvet as it curved around the balustrade until a staircase went in two directions. He took the stairs down a level to a concession stand that had a cleaned popcorn machine and candy in a glass case. He reached the lower balcony and wrapped his palms over the polished brass, rows of seats and the enormous empty bowl of the main room spread below. Hollow steps and the chatter of voices swirled up from the stage. Unknown to him or the rest of the group, Cob shifted his small body through the folds of the curtains, always watching and rarely seen.

Malcolm navigated a meandering hallway that let him out in a service kitchen. From there another switchback of stairs emptied onto the cavernous backstage. He came from behind a curtain to the left of the stage and stopped at his brother's side.

"Didn't this place burn down?" Malcolm asked, looking out at rows of dark seats.

"Twice," said Jordan, craning his neck at the Napoleonic cornices and restored crown moldings. "Dad played here, you know. I saw a picture of him at the house. He played live on television, a show called *Five Star Jubilee.*"

Malcolm faced Jordan until he looked over at him. "What are we doing here, Jordan?"

Jordan had sobered up and regained his wits. "I saw Uncle Jake yesterday."

"Wait, what?" It took Malcolm a minute. "I didn't know you guys talked."

"We don't. First time he seen my ass since we were in grade school. He was pretty hard to track down. I asked him why he and Dad don't talk no more. I don't know about you, but I never knew what really happened between them. They had some kind of falling out. I couldn't have asked Dad, he sure as shit wouldn't have told me. It was the only way."

Malcolm didn't say a word, he just shook his head. Some aspect hidden in him was revolted by speaking about the past in any regard, but especially as though it could be changed, or that there was anything at all to be gained by going back and revisiting it. He had worked hard to get where he was and Jordan was busy digging up what had long been buried. "Get to the point," he said.

"Jake blames Pa for killing our grandfather," said Jordan.

"Yeah, and how's that?"

"They were hunting in the mountains. Dad was supposed to clean up their campsite after dinner but left deer trimmings out by Grandpa's tent. A bear wandered into camp and mauled him. He bled out before they could get to a hospital, so Dad put him out right there in the backseat.

"I never knew why Jake stopped coming around, or how Grandpa died, come to think of it. Ever wonder why we know so little about what has really happened to this family? I'm no saint, I know, but look at us. Nobody talks to each other, we all live separate lives. Mom's dead, Dad's alone. We are scattered in the fallout of some tragedy none of us can recognize, let alone name."

"What the hell is going on with you?" Malcolm raised his voice. "You never used to give a shit about any of this. Dad, Uncle Jake, me. You are not going to put this picture back together again, Jordan—it's broken," Malcolm yelled. "It's been broken so long that it's the only way it's ever going to make any sense. Stop looking for something that isn't there. Move on, it's all we can do."

"Why does it piss you off so much?"

"Because I learned to live without you, Jordan. Just like you did without me or the rest of this family. You're a little late to the party. I know you know now, and I think that's great, but just because you know how truly awful you were, how disappointing it was to even look in your direction, that does not change how much hurt you caused. Just because you are now facing the heartache that befell our family, that doesn't change history. It won't make Dad and Jake inseparable again and it won't bring Grandpa back. Mom will not wake from where she sleeps. It won't change the years both of us were away. We don't get to choose when chaos finds its way into our lives. It just happens, and we persevere. There is no great understanding."

Jordan wandered to the opposite end of the stage, watching his friends kick their legs over the seats in the first balcony. Their watery image rumbled in his eyes. Malcolm followed him and Jordan wiped his arm over his face. "I would love to be able to move on, but I ain't like you. I have nothing to move on to. I have been walking away my entire life and it always leads to the same outcome." Jordan's voice grew hoarse and undone. "I won't emerge unscathed like you, perfect and whole. I am not whole," he yelled. "I have never been whole. Instead of wanting to die every moment I am awake, all I know how to do is be sorry. If that makes me weak, pathetic in your eyes, fine. That is all I have left, all the time in the world to learn what's been lost and fix what's been broken. What is left for me to do now is mend and do everything I can to stay in one place long enough to create something new that wasn't there before."

"I don't think you are pathetic," Malcolm assured him. He wrapped his arms around his brother. "But if I am being completely honest, I do think this is one of the most pathetic bachelor parties I have ever witnessed."

Jordan laughed, wiping his nose on his cuff.

"Now, can we go get drunk and lose our money like self-respecting men?"

Malcolm's bachelor party set out looking to gamble. Josh was least drunk among them and elected to drive. They got off the highway and crossed small wood bridges on languorous country roads scored over arms of water. They stepped out of Josh's car at the end of a dirt road beside a river whose gyres shifted in the darkness.

The Lucky Laurie was a riverboat casino moored outside the city in a tributary of the White River. Low-hanging coils of yellow bulbs cast a dull haze across the water and willows. It was certainly not New Orleans, or even Kansas City, but it would have to do. The Laurie had a storied past as one of many pleasure boats that popped up mysteriously in those waters offering game rooms, homemade booze, and local girls. No headlining act, not even a sign. When there was heat, either between competitors, or more likely raids from state agents, they would loose their moorings and drift further downriver, never to be caught in the same place twice. Men from neighboring counties were known to pay well for a solid hint at where the Laurie might stop to pick up new passengers. Before her there was Dick and Laramie's Bottoms Up Pontoon, whose portside at night read PLEASING TO THE EYE in broad red letters. In the forties, Bottoms Up competed with the Sun Bather and Mississippi Bend, who traded days of the week drifting the sandy road end where the boys had just arrived. One of the oldest boats, the Dame de Loisirs, captained by Mms. Elena Belle, an ex-madam from Metairie, kept a working alcohol still on board and a stable of pretty French and Creole girls. It used to have its own dock out back of Fred's Bait and Mortgage in Jefferson City and would crawl along Missouri river lines, drawing on a clientele of wholesome men and filth alike.

Obediah Cob knew it well. He waited until Malcolm, Jordan, and the boys filtered inside before making his way up the ramp. He drifted between crowded card tables and the farthest rows of quarter slots, keeping his delicate senses attuned to the brothers.

Violin and accordion music sighed under talking and steady drinking. Harrell, Russ, and Johnny found the bar. A waitress in a silk corset with cobalt lace took Baron by the arm and a grin spread across his face. "Hi sugar, my name is Julia. You need anything, you just let me know." She led him to a table in the corner.

Malcolm and Jordan found a blackjack table, where Jordan unfolded twenties on the felt and Malcolm removed his coat and placed it neat on the high back of the chair. He cracked his neck, stretched his hands, and rapidly counted a sequence of numbers on his fingers, recalling the game from memory. As Jordan divided their chips, he remembered Malcolm's ruthless talent for cards. Baron brought over beers and together they cheered one more time to his wedding, but Malcolm was already focused on the game. It would have been stupid for Jordan to stay at the table, the same as throwing money away. Plus, he hated losing to his brother, so he wished him well and set out on the floor.

Hours passed and Malcolm built himself a nice stack. He turned the table over not once but twice, bleeding down an over-weight Canadian woman and a man who never once looked up

from under the greasy curve of a NASCAR hat. He was feeling
good and barely noticed when the mild-tempered dealer left at the
end of her shift and was replaced by Lucius, a thin, harrowed man
with eyes of soot who ran his long fingers through the cards with
assured speed. The new dealer straightened his black vest, placed
two new decks in the caddy, and flung two cards to each player.
At first, the change was slight. Malcolm noticed the quality of
his hands decline so he backed off a bit, content to play conser-
vatively until his cards improved. After a while, no ideal opening
arose for him to get back into the game. Lucius turned hands at
a blinding rate and made the table unapproachable, regardless of
the moves he made. His chip count lingered around two thousand,
impressive in just a few hours, but now he was concerned with
protecting what he had earned. A waitress brought him a scotch
and soda. He placed a two-dollar chip on her tray and she dragged
the tips of her nails across the top of his hand.

Lucius raised his brow and asked him what he thought of her.

"Cute girl," said Malcolm.

"That's a hot little piece of ass, especially for this place," Lucius said. "I can hook you up, just say the word."

Malcolm looked around to find the highback chairs next to
him empty, save a pasty twenty-something in a Tapout T-shirt
rocking his head to the treble hissing through his headphones.
"I've got a date to be married," Malcolm said, swallowing his dis-
taste. "Thanks though."

"More for me, then. I used to fuck all the girls at the Queen,
you know in KC? Dumber 'an dirt, most of 'em. The Queen caught
me skimming, happens all the time. E'rybody does it, but they like
to act like they don't know. It was one of them bitches that rat-
ted me out. She found out I had got with her friend. Somehow,
I got out of there with only a censure from the Commission."

He looked around before leaning in close. "Then I landed here, middle of nowhere, talking to a guy like you about banging middle-of-the-road ass like that. Oh, how the mighty have fallen. No offense," said Lucius.

Malcolm cleared eighty and threw him ten, hoping it would shut him up.

"Obliged," he said. "So, you're tying the knot. I ain't never doing that again, shit. Last girl I was serious on cheated first chance she got. This pill-poppin' motherfucker that lived on her block. Talking 'bout she addicted, she need help. I went over there one night, told him to crawl his ass out the house and face me like a man, you know. He came out with a gun, so I ran back up in my house and got my fucking gun. My girl run in screaming. I said your dope dick boyfriend out there started it. Go on run over there, I told her. Right then a shot came through the window. I hit the light in the living room and we dropped to our stomachs on broken glass. She yelled for him to get on, that someone was gone get hurt. We was crawling around and she lays into me right there. Can you believe that? How I don't amount to nothing, how I never finished college, put all my money into racing cars, lost my job at the casino. That's when I said, ain't no woman going to tell me what I'm worth. Next day I told her so long. Might have ended up in this forsaken hole, but I got my dignity."

Malcolm had lost four hands in a row and leveled off with one that finally beat Lucius. He continued raising Malcolm's ire. "You'll see. Last thing you ever think will happen, one day you wake up and that shit is your life. You can be a man, face up to all you done, or do what I did and run. Question is, do you still got nuts below the table. Looking at you, I bet you do. But what you don't see coming will lay you low in the end. Best keep them eyes open, killer."

After leaving his brother at the blackjack table, Jordan foundered his way through a few rounds of roulette and backed away from the wheel, sure of his unlucky hand. Malcolm had once told him that he was too impulsive and easily provoked to gamble. Judging by the fact that the comment still echoed through his mind years later, he might have had a point. At least he was not cold and calculating like his brother, the robot, Jordan assured himself as he mindlessly tapped the screen of a video poker machine at the bar. Time passed, the money went, and Jordan pried himself away, annoyed.

As he stumbled across the carpeted floor, he was assaulted by the onslaught of ringing bells and flashing lights. He found a port door and pushed his way outside, pulling the night air in through his nose, exhaling big, deep breaths. It wasn't only bad luck and noisy lights that were getting to him. He had never tried to explain it to anyone before, but he went through periods of increasing discomfort. These episodes were normal after he had done something wrong, especially if he had hurt himself or someone else, and struggled to bring the tide of anxiety and guilt under his control. But when he had not done anything excessive or violent, he was caught off guard. He grew increasingly hot, skin pricked by needles, his mind racing and paranoid. Jordan flinched and checked over both shoulders, making sure he wasn't being watched. There was never anybody there, but he could not shake the intuitive sense that at his most vulnerable, when he was all alone and calm enough to let his guard down, he couldn't do so pinned beneath someone's prying gaze.

The deck of the Lucky Laurie was lined with benches and small tables where couples huddled together, sipped drinks and talked. Walking to the front of the bow, Jordan saw a woman staring into the water, her face turned away to hide her sobbing. He asked if she was okay. When there was no response he remained at her side, assuming she hadn't heard the question. The wind blew on the wide open deck, he leaned closer and asked again. Her damp, reddened face rose in the opaque halo of the lanterns strung over the railing. He sat beside her on the bench. Jordan reached out and placed his hand gently on her back.

She turned to him and stalled her crying enough to speak. "I lost someone important to me, a year ago this weekend," she told him. "My friends forced me to come here tonight. They were just trying to cheer me up, I know. It worked for a while, but I couldn't take it in there, all the lights and the noise and cigarette smoke."

"I know what you mean," said Jordan.

The woman examined Jordan's face. "He was a lot like you. Handsome, a wounded sort of boy. You two would have been roughly the same age, I imagine." She clutched his hand, again breaking into tears. An unwillingly howl rose from her throat as though she had been stabbed in the gut. Jordan closed his eyes.

"I was running late that day, always in such a rush," she cursed herself. "If I had not been so selfish, he wouldn't have been hit, he would still be here." She let another howl pour over the bow. "Pieces of him were on the road. The police asked me to identify him, but how was I supposed to recognize pieces? You know, the weak bear the burden while killers go free. God is not just. They say he is, but it's not true. He is vengeful, petty, spurned by his ire, exactly what the commandments were passed to Moses to warn us against." She wiped the run from her nose and clutched hold of Jordan. "So my son is taken from me and I am left to rot. Still, I'll pray for him as long as I can. I don't need anyone to pray for me, it's too late for that. Pray for yourself, young man, that you see your way clear of this treachery. Ask yourself, am I ready for what the devils have in store?"

———

Malcolm washed his face in the sink, changed out of his collared shirt, and secured his money in the safe at the foot of the closet. He had cashed out fifteen hundred in chips from the teller and brought the winnings back to the room in a shopping bag. Jordan stretched out on the other double and switched on the television. He sat up and rummaged around in his bag until he surfaced a bottle of bourbon.

"Travel with the essentials, I see," said Malcolm.

"I'm going to get some ice," Jordan replied. He flipped the plastic bucket in his hands.

"If I doze off—"

"I'll just hit you in the face, real hard."

Malcolm was already closing his eyes, adrift. The television murmured updates from an explosion at a fertilizer plant and alerts about a coming storm. The room fell still, a soothing pattern of rain on the window that aided Malcolm's sleep until he shot up in bed, heart pounding, startled by a woman's scream. He heard it a second time and discerned that it came from the end of the hall before it was muffled by sounds of a struggle. Bodies shuffled and strained, two loud bangs followed by silence. The commotion led Malcolm to a metal door with a glowing red emergency sign adjacent to the last room on the floor. He banged his fist below room number 212. A man's voice swore, then Malcolm heard a heavy piece of furniture being dragged across the carpet. He banged again, jumping back as the door flew open. Russ breathed heavy, intense with menace.

"Let me in, Russ."

"Man, go back to your room and mind your own busin—"

Malcolm took one step back and kicked the door straight into Russ's forehead. He fell on the floor and Malcolm rushed into the room, wired with adrenaline. A faint girl lay topless on the bed, rocking with pain. He drew her hair to one side and discovered the blood that stained her nose and lips, still fresh from a wound Russ had no doubt caused. Malcolm tried to get her to sit up but stopped when she went stiff and cried out in agony. He felt her clammy forehead and asked if she was hurt anywhere else. Nearly unresponsive, she managed to shake her head.

He stood from the bed and found a tray strewn with weed and cut-up pills on the dresser where Russ's survival knife sat, unfolded. Malcolm's eyes went from the knife to Russ, who did the same to him, assessing the danger they posed to each other. Both men lunged forth, but Malcolm got there first. He secured the grooved handle and turned it on Russ, who gripped his wrist with his one good hand before Malcolm slammed him against the wall. Malcolm screwed a fistful of flannel into Russ's chest, smashed him twice and finally pinned him there with the gruesome blade to his throat.

"Move and I'll cut your other arm off," he warned. The polished metal wavered above the rough skin pulsing at his neck. "How about it? Care to test me? If that girl wasn't drugged and beat so bad, I would just hand her the knife, see what she'd fix to do with it. Maybe she'd have purpose to cut your balls off. What do you think, Russ? Would you miss them more than your arm?"

Russ fell silent with fear. He swallowed hard, sweat ran down his cheek.

"Let's wait here together just like this and see if she comes around," said Malcolm. "I got no other plans."

The commotion had roused Harrell and the rest of the boys a few doors down. They poured in through the open doorway and filled the room. "What's going on? You lost your mind, Malcolm?" Harrell grasped to make sense of the situation.

"Seems Russ here had the virtuous plan of drugging and raping one of the girls from downstairs. Check to see if she's all right, will you?"

Baron held her jaw up and braced the back of her neck to check her breathing. She was out cold. "Oh, shit," he muttered. "She's a waitress. Julia, that's her name."

Baron sat Julia upright, but when he removed his hand from propping her up she fell backward on the bed, eyelids thick and blue. He draped her limp arm over his shoulder and anchored her against the headboard of the bed, where she managed to stay up.

Jordan had returned with the ice to find his own room empty, so he followed the shouting. He came in, smoothed back his hair, and studied the pills on the table.

"Goddamn it, Russ."

"Jordan, listen, you know me. Tell your brother to calm down. He's got it all wrong."

Malcolm pressed the knife into a large contracting vein. Russ tried his luck and struggled once more, but Malcolm was planted firm and could not be moved. He curled his knuckles and punched him with the knife hand, spattering blood across the wallpaper. He rubbed his fist into Russ's teeth and smeared blood across his face in a red cloud.

"You want to die?" he said. "Move one more time."

Jordan could sense his brother growing angrier as he examined every sweating pore on Russ's sorry face. "How easy it would be to end this piece of shit," Malcolm reasoned. "What would be lost? The world would be better off." The more he considered it, the less he found fundamentally wrong with killing Russ.

"The situation is under control, Malcolm. Come on, end this." Jordan pleaded with his brother, but to Malcolm the calls were far away, signals jumping the chasm from another realm.

Malcolm spit as he addressed the terrified Russ. "What if I just did it, though? Have you thought about what it would be like to have all your blood rush out of your body?" He pressed the tip of the blade into one sunken point in his neck. "If you knew you only had one moment left to live, if you were given that gift of knowing you were about to die, what would be your last thought? I wouldn't waste this precious time, if I was you."

"I always knew you were an evil fuck," Russ managed to get out. "You turned your back on your brother, everything you came from. You're a rich wannabe, no better than the rest of us. No lie you tell yourself can change that, Malcolm. Remember that."

Julia had woken and Baron and Josh rushed to move her to the hallway, where she vomited. Baron held a cold towel on her forehead and poured small sips of water into her mouth. Josh told her that they were going to get her to a hospital.

The rain beat the window behind the curtain. "Let go of him," Jordan begged. "The girl's going to get help. You are getting married, for Christ's sake. That's why we are here, Malcolm. Think of Elizabeth."

The overhead light and the lamp on the bureau went dim and the air around Malcolm collapsed in an absence of light. In that flash, Jordan was looking in the mirror when he saw Malcolm's eyes go black. His brother's reflection doubled and then there were two of him standing side by side. The skin on his face and arms was shocked white like the ash from a fire. Darkness spread from his pupils and grew in deep hues around his eyes and mouth. The lights flickered in the room and in those flashes Malcolm's bare chest was covered with strange markings.

The power surged and brilliant light spread throughout the room. Malcolm's eyes flipped back to normal and darted over to meet Jordan's horrified stare in the mirror. As they looked at each other, the surface of the glass began to creak. Lines spread to each corner and split the mirror with a loud crack, glass falling in shards.

Malcolm lowered his arm and released Russ. Staring off with a vacant, empty gaze, he walked up to Jordan and dropped the knife in his hand.

THIRTEEN

JORDAN THREW WATER OVER his face and bare chest and returned to Leah's bed to watch the vaporous clouds dissipate after last night's storm. Leah received his call after work, too tired to raise her guard. At first, she wasn't going to answer. She had already started to hate him less, but it was still not natural for him to enter her mind without being torn to shreds. She stared at his boots untied and kicked on the floor, then watched him lie beside her on the bed. Even still, he was like a wounded animal. He would shrink away from her when they talked, sit on the farthest end of the couch, keep himself contained and quarantine his body, careful not to afflict or infect her. She was reminded of her rescued lab, Louise, when she was just a puppy. When Leah first brought Louise home, she sat sleepy-eyed with her head in the corner, her thin brown coat quaking with fear, doing her best not to attract anyone's attention. It took days for Leah to draw her out of that corner, weeks to get her to recognize what kindness looked like, and months for her to trust that it would not be ripped away.

Leah admitted she had built Jordan into somewhat of a monster, a villain comprised of hurt and embittered passions he was mostly not responsible for. Now to touch his worn skin and kiss his tough lips, she fought against it still. She resented that wounded distance of his because it was her defense as well and she was not

used to someone else lumbering around with it. She had confront-
ed being alone, but she was not prepared to face how ordinary
her anger actually was. Leah had been angry her entire life and the
thought of losing that anger terrified her. She broke into a low cry
and scooped herself onto the breast of the boy she loved to rage
against, who had vanished and returned, not denying anything,
accepting everything, her only possession the quiet demeanor of
the survivor that forced her to admit, rather simply, that whatever
she had faced in life, she too had survived. She too would be okay.
Leah wept with consuming rapture. Not against a ruinous force,
or a familiar bereave, but for the first time yearning to let go toward the unknown, instead of letting it scare her to death.

She swallowed gulps of air as though she had surfaced from a
well and wandered around her house touching surfaces to various
parts of her body—couch fabric to her thighs, the plastic television
remote to her forehead, the hewn curves of Jordan's fingers on her
breasts. Long-obstructed passages in her began to break until she
exploded. They wrapped their bodies around each other so tight the
air squeezed out of her lungs. A trail of clothes littered the way to
her bedroom, where they cried and laughed and pushed into each
other, tending to the invisible sites of each other's wounds.

When they woke that afternoon, Leah made coffee and listened as Jordan told her about the confrontation between Russ
and his brother at the Lucky Laurie. She never knew Malcolm well,
but knowing he was Jordan's twin, she was not all that surprised.
"The guy with one arm," she said. "He was going to rape that poor
girl?" Jordan nodded. "So your brother did the right thing, then."

"I have never seen him do anything like that before."

Leah's laugh blew steam from her cup of coffee. "He's a
Bayne, Jordan. When it comes down to it y'all do the right thing,
just in the wrong way. You can't help it, it's in your blood."

"That's always been my way, though, not his. I was dumb, he was smart. He followed the rules, I broke them. I used my hands, he used his brain. I went through life like a freight train and he slipped by undetected. My Pa told me once that I always went straight through him, never around. I didn't know what that meant until much later. But Malcolm was different. He steered clear of us all. It was like he was playing by a different set of rules that only he knew."

"That could just be his nature," Leah said. Jordan asked what she meant. "You built your brother into this alter ego, who is smarter and faster than you, always one step ahead, but he grew up the same way you did. I mean, he might not have known that's what he was doing, it was just the way it came out. I bet there is a lot he doesn't know about himself. You're not perfect but neither is he, so don't take it so hard. Stop putting the suffering of the world on your shoulders. Jesus did that already—it'd be vain for you to even try."

Jordan smiled. She kissed his chin.

"Now get them jeans on," she said. "We have to go buy a new washer."

Malcolm was on his hands and knees with his nose in the dirt. "Look at these flowers," he said, annoyed. "The caterers keep trampling back and forth through here. God forbid people be mindful of their fucking actions." He raised his voice knowing Elizabeth was behind him watching him hold the withered pedals. She bent down and wrapped her arms around his navy shirt damp with sweat. When he was upset, he projected static, concocting a buffer of space around him as he shifted from one frenetic activity to the next as a distraction. Elizabeth hated when it got all over her.

"You don't have to tell me," she said, "but did something happen last night? I know you said you had a good time, but you're my baby, Malcolm— I can tell when you're upset." Elizabeth kissed a spot of salt from Malcolm's neck. He pulled away and returned his focus to the garden bed. She closed her eyes against the sun, then opened them to watch a butterfly with white wings hover over the rows of flowers like it was doting on a string. She asked again about the party.

"I told you, nothing happened." Malcolm worked his arms in the dirt and recounted how they drove to Springfield to pick up Jordan.

"I thought you were going to New Orleans?"

"He was drunk, upset about something our uncle told him, so we said what the hell and went out up there."

"Wait," Elizabeth said, shielding her eyes. "What uncle?"

"Jordan found our uncle Jake living up that way. He sought him out, I guess he wanted to know the truth about something that happened a long time ago." Malcolm grunted as he dug into the earth, twisting the soil. When he was not forthcoming with more details from the trip, Elizabeth grunted herself. "All right, fine," he said. "He wanted to know why my dad and Uncle Jake don't talk and Jake told him it's because he blames Walker for killing our grandfather, Maurel."

That was not what Elizabeth expected him to say. She asked if there was any truth to the claim.

"Who can know for sure? I'm supposed to believe Jake, who I haven't seen since I was a boy?" He quit laboring and closed one eye to stop the sting of invading sweat. "It's Jordan whose drudging all this up, not me. There's a lot I don't know, and I don't need to know. I don't know why he can't let this go, but it's starting to piss me off." Malcolm stabbed his trowel in the dirt. "This family will be the death of me, I swear."

"He told me he's been thinking about the past, how things went. He just wants some closure. Is that so bad?" Elizabeth asked in earnest.

Malcolm inched the dirty yard gloves from his hands and climbed to his feet. "Everything my brother touches turns to shit. How do you not understand that yet? I don't know why he is getting into this nonsense and I don't care. People he never knew, things that have nothing to do with him that no one can change anyhow. Like I said, it's best forgotten, that's what the past is for. If he keeps on about this it's going to blow up in his face. He won't know what to do, he never does. But he will deserve it."

They trudged back in the house and Malcolm washed a stream of brown water from his hands and watched the dirt circle down the drain. "Trust me," he told Elizabeth. "You'll see."

"So, that's it?"

Malcolm poured a cup of lemonade from the pitcher on the counter and took a long sip, holding the cold glass to the sweaty side of his cheek.

"I would love some lemonade," she said. "Thank you, honey." Elizabeth grabbed a glass and filled it herself.

"There's more," he said. Malcolm proceeded to tell her about Jordan breaking into the theater and how the evening took a turn at the casino. Elizabeth gasped and covered her mouth when he told her about the unconscious girl and his fight with Russ. "They got the girl to a hospital, thank God. I let him go, but I was angry, Elizabeth. I mean real anger. Then I realized what I was doing and let him go." Malcolm paused and chose his words carefully. "This place does bad things to people."

Elizabeth folded her arms across her chest. "You mean to you," she said. "It does bad things to you."

"Everyone hates where they are from, it's a fact."

"Not me," Elizabeth countered. "I don't hate where I am from."

"You're from the Outer Banks—that doesn't count. The longer we stay, the more I am reminded of why I left."

"Well, please try and make it until our wedding. You know, if
that suits you." Elizabeth slammed her glass on the counter and
stormed out of the kitchen, stomping each step on her way upstairs.

"Y'all got Target now? Moving up in the world, I see." Jordan
pulled his truck into a newly paved lot filled with rows of parked
cars shining in the midday sun. Leah dug smokes out of her purse
and lit two, handing Jordan one as they walked across the massive
parking lot. "Texas has anything you could ever want, but it took
two hours to get anywhere. My friends thought where we're from
was country, they're ones to talk."

"Is it country down there? I never been," said Leah.

"Not San Antonio, that's for sure. The desert's all right. I tend
to like places with the least amount of people. There's a bunch of
ugly buildings, big highways, sky, desert, then Mexico."

In the shining depths of a huge corridor lined with cheap
products, Jordan pulled blouses and dresses off the racks and held
them below Leah's chin. She blushed and whacked a blue one with
white flowers on the lapel from his hand. "You need a dress that
rivals how pretty you are," he told her.

"New and improved Jordan, same bullshit charm. What am I
going to do with a thing like that?" she asked.

"I'll take you somewhere. To the theater," Jordan said.

Leah laughed, she rubbed the soft fabric between her fingers.
"Do you even know where there is a theater? Besides, this is a
summer dress. That's why it's on clearance, they want to get rid
of it."

"Hang on to it," Jordan said. "For the future."

"We came in here for a washing machine." She nodded down
the aisle. They stood in front of a wall of washer-dryers and picked
out the one Leah saw in the seasonal mailer, which they paid for

and loaded into the truck. Jordan pushed the heavy box all the way into the bed and strapped it down.

A flash of birds broke from the cluster of trees across the street. They shot apart and dove back together in unison before fading into another canopy. An alarm began to howl from a car on the other end of the parking lot. Jordan scoured the sea of cars and looked right below where the birds had passed. There was a Civic emanating the shrill wave of sound, and next to it Jordan spotted a peculiar-looking Cadillac Fleetwood. Nobody came running, fumbling their keys to stop the alarm. Jordan thought it was odd, so he kept an eye on it. A man in a camouflaged hat circled for a spot to park his Camaro. A fat teenager drew from her cigarette and squinted at Jordan while holding a sun-bleached baby doll by its ankle. That was when Jordan saw someone ducking below the steering wheel of the Fleetwood, staring back at him.

Leah finished cinching straps around the washer in the back and waited for Jordan to get in the truck. He started the ignition and let his breath across the dashboard, pensive. He could not have explained it to Leah, he was barely aware of it himself, but Jordan knew he was being watched. It was as though he knew who was going to be in the car before he saw him sitting there. The draw of the man hiding in the white Cadillac was magnetic. Had Jordan seen him before? If he was being honest, he had felt the same piercing gaze upon him ever since he stepped out the door in San Antonio, though he had not been aware of it until that moment. His mind went clear, body shot with nerves.

Leah asked, "What's the matter?"

"See that white car back there, the Cadillac?" He pointed across the rows. "There is a man in the car looking at us. I think he has been following me for a while."

"Don't you think you're going too far with this stuff?" Leah asked.

Obediah Cob crouched behind the wheel of the Cadillac, unsure whether or not Jordan had seen him. He sat still trying not to move, but when Jordan let his truck idle for an inordinately long time, Cob was sure his cover had been blown. He tilted the brim of his hat above his eyes and quickly threw the Fleetwood into gear, wheeling around the opposite way through the exit.

Jordan and Leah watched as the car sped out of the lot.

"Okay, now you're freaking me out." Leah craned her neck to get a look before Cob piloted the Fleetwood out of sight.

The ignition grumbled while Jordan weighed his options. "Know what? Fuck this." Jordan was fixed on the direction Cob had sped. "It's time to find out what the hell is going on."

Paced back on the road, Jordan followed the Cadillac. The lights at the center of town dissipated into the spectral spans of Felson Woods and the road wound from two lanes to a single, dimly lit path. Buildings and developments turned to dilapidated ruins that sagged by the roadside. Heavy green obscured what unknown bounds lay beyond.

Leah lived on the far side of the nearest town but had never ventured out this far, for obvious reasons. She could not believe what they were doing, descending into the backwoods alone, chasing a phantom. She knew Jordan was not going to change his mind, not now. She kicked her foot up on the dash and sulked in her seat. The trees took over and civilization decayed out her window.

After meandering miles of woods they turned on a dirt road called Iron Mire. They wound down a shallow hillside that leveled out across the valley floor. It was like moving backward in time, Old Chevys tarped on blocks, their back halves chopped off. A wagon sat abandoned in the gulley of a ditch, windows busted, vegetation bursting through corroded floor panels, vines climbing out of the spidered windshield. Mounds of hay and garbage were piled high in the fields. An emaciated dog slept in a cracked plastic swimming pool. When the truck slowed around a bend, they passed a collapsed barn painted with the American flag. In the stripes were tall letters that spelled out, GET U.S. OUT OF THE U.N., and Leah spied an effigy of Obama hanging from a tree by a noose, shot through with half a dozen arrows and rotted from years of rain.

"Jesus," Leah muttered against the fogged window.

"Do you know where we are?" Jordan asked.

"I don't get out this way very often, if you can imagine." She checked the dim display of her phone. "Great, there's no reception."

They had fallen far behind Cob, the teardrops of the Fleetwood's taillights no longer visible. Trees choked out daylight and cooled the air. A pit pried opened Jordan's stomach. Something didn't feel right. The sureness he set out with in town had turned to anticipation and worry. He had no way of knowing where the car went, or what he would do if he somehow found him. He glanced at Leah, cursing himself for involving her, then he cracked the window and took deep breaths of air mixed with cigarette smoke.

Jordan slowed at a fork. There was no one else in sight. Leah waited for his next move as he fought to dispel a rising negative tide. The shrill call of crows filled his mind. He looked around. The birds remained hidden but Jordan listened closely to their song. The murder was calling from the north, farther down the road that bent to the right of the fork. Leah was relieved they were moving again. She craned her neck and barely caught the lithe black bodies of birds hovering together over a tall stand of pines. "Over there," she yelled. More ravens swooped in to form

a continuous, revolving circle. Jordan drove slowly through heavy
forest, cautiously spying the shanties at the roadside. A mile in on
the road, he spotted the back end of the Cadillac parked beside a
cabin. He pulled the truck alongside some heavy brush and killed
the engine. He got out and approached on foot. Jordan raced
alongside the trees, past a portage covered with moss, and came
to a stop below a small window. He leaned against the wall of the
cabin and caught his breath, watching the cord of gray that rose
from the chimney stones.

A dark rock sat adorned with strange markings drawn in white
chalk above Andridge Grieves' mantelpiece. At the center, a large
circle was struck through with four lines, summoning each cardi-
nal direction. Through a small side window, Jordan thought the
circle resembled a target. On one end, two dots filled the ends of a
horizontal X, on the other an egg was cracked open by a bolt of
lightning. Stacks of dots along the bottom were arranged in sets
of interconnected triangles. They were marked with the characters of
a language Jordan could not understand. The circle in the center
was made up of seven smaller concentric circles. At each sight of
their intersection was placed an astrological symbol, one for each
house of the zodiac. To the right was a list of dates, times, and
locations that pertained to the Bayne family.

Jordan cupped his hand over glass and squinted into the cabin.
He was unable to comprehend most of what he saw, but in reading the list of dates and times he recognized the date of his and
his brother's birth. There was also a map with a pin on the location
of the motor court where Jordan lived in San Antonio. If he had a
hunch before, his curiosity was full-blown concern now.

Cob came into the room. It was the first time Jordan had gotten a clear look at him. His face sat pudgy and fat beneath the

curled brim of his bowler and a vested tan suit. A larger presence passed close in front of the window, causing Jordan to shrink back and duck in the grass. The looming body lowered into the leather chair beside the fireplace, and Jordan saw a wraith of an enormously tall man stroking the cloudy strands of his beard while flipping through the densely annotated pages of Cob's notebook. Jordan guessed he stood almost seven feet tall, which was why the writing on the slate was up so high above the fire. His gray whiskers and beard hung like strings of moss from an ancient tree. His movements were slight but deliberate, as though everything he did was of great importance. Jordan could not help but recall the local lore, stories passed down as kids, about a giant who stalked the hills and preyed on children, elusive as a ghost. Never for a second did Jordan ever consider that he could be real.

Andridge Grieves sat beside the fire, pushed a thumb full of tobacco into a briar pipe, and lit it. Jordan could barely make out what was being discussed, but he heard Andridge ask Cob if they had returned from Missouri yet.

"Yes, Andridge, early yesterday morning. There could be a problem, though." Cob was reluctant, almost scared. "I sat on the kid at a shopping center. When they came back out, he may have seen me."

Cob kept talking but Andridge cut him off. "How could you be so reckless? Were you just sitting out in the open?"

"Of course not," Cob said, vehement in his denial. "It was a busy parking lot. To be honest, I don't know how he saw me. The kid is keen."

"This has the potential for trouble." Grieves' voice was like ripped paper. "Should I be troubled, Obediah?"

"No sir, I will handle it."

"Good. The father is almost ready, anyway. It is close now, we mustn't interfere. I'm concerned about our proximity. We may

now be exposed, thanks to you. No more close calls, got it?" Andridge cleared his throat and Cob disappeared into the kitchen,
returning with a mug of tea. He asked if Andridge needed anything more. "I will be fine. Where is everyone now?" he asked.

"The watcher is staying close, with the bride and her family at
a nearby hotel. Walker is at home," Cob assured him.

"When's the wedding?"

"Tomorrow night."

"It will be done by then, I am sure of it." Andridge sipped
his tea.

Cob tilted his head back and began humming in soft inter-
vals, letting the language of the earth swirl through his senses.
Andridge looked on with interest from his rocking chair as Cob
walked to the head of the cabin and opened the front door, his
peculiar shadow stretched by a halo of porch light. Jordan crept
a few steps back to the far side of the cabin as Cob stepped into
the grass after him, emanating the same two-tone pattern, trying
to locate him through song. When Cob turned the corner, though,
he found nothing but the wind.

FOURTEEN

IN ROOM SIXTEEN OF the Seven Pines Motel, Jordan paced in front
of a closed burgundy curtain. A television beat the room with a
kaleidoscope of State Little League championships, failed trans-
portation bills, and four thousand birds falling out of the sky in
Ono. Jordan switched to the weather, where a sun wearing black
sunglasses baked Newton County in sizzling waves for the rest
of the weekend, with the exception of one frowning cloud that
cried raindrops from its eyes. He muted the volume and tuned in a
George Jones song through the static on the wood-paneled radio.
He took a seat at the round table and poured a healthy amount of
bourbon into a Styrofoam cup from the coffee maker, assessing
the seriousness of what he had just done.

The frail body of Andridge Grieves lay slumped over, his long
arms and legs duct-taped to a chair. Grieves had photographs and
personal information. There were symbols, esoteric markings,
charts that detailed the passage of the planets around the sun. He
and Cob had meticulously tracked Jordan's entire family for God
knew how long or for what purpose. They knew intimate details
about members of the Bayne family that Jordan never even knew
existed. They spoke of things that he had just done, like talking
to his uncle in Mountain Home. They even knew what they had
talked about. Nobody could have known that except Jacob and his

brother. They were fixated on Malcolm and Elizabeth's wedding. He had heard Andridge talk about his father's whereabouts as well, and he knew he had heard Cob tell him that the time was close. The time was close for what? Jordan rolled the question around in his head, which only made him angrier and more suspicious. He came to the conclusion that Andridge and Cob were planning to kill Walker, though he had no idea why. Regardless of the reason, Jordan resolved that there was no way he was going to let that happen.

"You are going to tell me who you are and what you want with my family," said Jordan.

"I want nothing from you or your loved ones," Andridge said. "I am merely a custodian."

"There's pictures, maps, my birthday on a damn star chart."

Andridge smirked with half his mouth.

"How long has that little man been following me?"

"He goes by Cob, Obediah Cob. I assure you, he never intended malice. He only watched you for as long as was necessary."

"What does that mean, necessary?"

"You are involved in a kind of process. The scope of which even I am unsure. I am caught up in it myself, you see."

"Caught up in what?"

"A process," Andridge repeated.

Jordan lunged forward and punched him hard in the face. "Speak plain fucking English."

"I am. You're not hearing it, boy. You are going around pulling together all these different pieces, hoping to figure it out, but all of the pieces will always add up to less than one because you are the missing piece. You are at the center. You think you've been lost your whole life. You are not lost, Jordan. You are right where you need to be. Funny, you consider yourself living by your own devices, making your own way, nobody caring whether you live or die. I know you want to do something, feel you must act. You sense danger but don't know why. You are not supposed to know."

"You don't know a thing about me," Jordan said.

"I know the prospect of perishing brings everyone closer together."

Jordan stormed onto the second-story balcony, shuffled down the stairs, unlocked his truck, and leaned across the seat to retrieve his gun from the glove box. He marched back upstairs into the room and pointed it at Andridge. "Now," he said. "If you don't tell me why you are planning to kill my father, I am going to shoot you in the face. Right here, right now. Your choice." Jordan leaned over Andridge, his head bowed forward in the chair. He gripped the .38 to reinforce his ultimatum. "Better start talking."

Andridge hung his head and sighed. "Fine," he said. "I hoped it wouldn't come to this." Grieves raised his eye at Jordan. "I am not going to kill your father. Your brother is."

At the Bayne house, Malcolm returned from a late run. After dinner with Elizabeth and his soon-to-be mother-in-law, he discovered two missed calls from Jordan on his phone, calls that had spanned the last ten hours.

Elizabeth laid on the bed upstairs and pulled her legs on top of the sheets. "It's too muggy. I had too much wine at dinner, too much of everything," she said, faint. Malcolm took off her shoes, smoothed the damp hair at her forehead, and wrestled her under the covers. He told her to get some rest, then climbed from the bed and pulled a jacket from the closet.

"Where are you going?" she asked.

"For a drive, need to clear my head. I'll be back in a little while. You get your beauty rest, it's our big day tomorrow." Malcolm told her he loved her, turned out the light, and closed the door.

The roadside parsed aged ruins across rolling acreage. Abandoned farms, grist mills, horse stalls, and outbuildings collapsed into the ground like discarded skeletons. Houses hid away behind stunted hickory and slash pine. Many of the farms had long ceased operation, disenfranchised by the new economy, but those that still clung to life limped into the twenty-first century any way they could. He came to the intersection at Buffalo Creek Road and pulled up the short driveway in front of Leah Fayette's house. After two knocks, she peeked through the drapes and cracked open the door.

"Hi there, Leah. I'm Malcolm, Jordan's brother."

"I know who you are. Would you like to come in?" she asked.

"No, that's all right. Sorry to disturb you so late. Normally I wouldn't be so impolite, but—"

"But I'm guessing this has to do with your brother."

"I missed two calls from him today, which is more than he's called me in ten years. Usually, he's not even one to use a phone. It's got me worried. Have you seen or heard from him?"

Leah stepped barefoot onto the step and the screen door clapped behind her. "Not since yesterday, when he went all crazy."

"Crazy how? He wasn't still drinking, was he?"

"No, nothing like that. We were at Target picking up a washing machine for the house here. We came out of the store and Jordan swore he saw someone in an old car, watching us. I asked him what was up. He recognized him, said he had seen him before. I didn't think much of it, but then we got on the road and I realized we weren't coming back here. Ended up following the dirty ass end of that Cadillac for over an hour. I'm telling you, this place was way out there. Gave me a bad feeling."

"Do you know where you ended up?" he asked.

"Way out on 16 West, we pulled off the main road and there were no signs after that. Followed some dirt road and came to a stop outside a cabin set way back in the woods, I couldn't really see much."

"Did anything happen?" Malcolm asked her.

"I stayed in the truck while he crept around looking in windows. I don't know what the hell he was doing. When he came back to the truck, I told him if we didn't get out of there that minute he could find his own way home because I was gone leave his sorry ass for the coyotes."

"So that was it, huh," said Malcolm.

"He dropped me off back here all by myself with the washer, then he left again. Knowing him, he probably went back," Leah said.

She and Malcolm leaned against the thin metal railing, ruminating on what Jordan could have gotten himself into. Leah reached into the pocket of her hooded sweatshirt and unwrapped the plastic on a new pack and lit a Marlboro Light. Malcolm stretched his back, looking at the houses across the street, then both ways down the deserted road.

"I'm telling you, the whole thing was strange," she continued. "One minute we're making up, shopping, being fucking affectionate. Next I know we're hightailing it down some back road to God knows where." She pulled on her cigarette, incensed. "There was nothing I could say, and whatever he saw in that cabin only made it worse."

Malcolm thanked her and walked back to his car when she called out to him. "Congratulations, by the way."

"What?" Malcolm asked.

"On getting married," she said.

"Oh right, that." Malcolm leaned on his opened door. "I'll have him call you when I find him."

"Yeah," Leah said. "I'll hold my breath."

As dusk turned to night, a nearby field danced with flashes from a brush pile set ablaze. Shirtless bodies half-submerged in dark hauled heavy stalks out of the woods. One of them swung an axe, splitting deadfall that the others dragged across the ground and heaved on top of the flames. A plume of sparks cascaded against an old house and burned out in the sky. Men with scars on their stomachs stared from the corner of the yard. As Malcolm approached, two of them walked into the road sipping cans of Busch. The skinny one took a few steps up the pavement and lifted the dirty metal of a shotgun toward Malcolm's car. The drunk clinched one eye closed to aim down the barrel and lost his balance, staggering off the roadside. Malcolm glared in the rearview as he gained control of the car.

Slumberland was a bar nestled in the shell of an old mattress store that would have appeared abandoned were it were not for the cars angled in front and shadows curled around glowing cigarettes huddled together in clouds of smoke. Malcolm found Jordan at the far end of the bar, not so much nursing a pint as having a deep conversation with one.

"Thought I'd find you here," said Malcolm.

Jordan patted the seat of an open stool. "Yeah, and how'd you come by that?"

"Same spot I found you the last time nobody knew where you were, after you beat Carl Reese with a shovel and he came tearing after you."

Jordan let out a hiccup of laughter. "Never did catch me. I'm good at hiding, tired as I am of it."

The bartender brought Malcolm a light draught. He sipped the white foam off the top of his glass. "So," he said.

"So, what?"

"Don't fuck with me, Jordan." Malcolm glanced down the barroom in the direction of the door. "Where's your truck?" he asked. "I didn't see it outside."

"I walked."

"What're we doing here?"

"I've been thinking about Mom." He gulped a pocket of air and stacked it in his gut. "How is it I can be sharp as a tack with a list of shit I'd love to forget, but when it comes to dear old Mercy Bayne I can't remember a damn thing?"

"We were young, it was cancer. People die of it every day. I see it at work constantly. People work hard, keep their hopes raised, do their best to handle it as it comes, but whatever is meant to happen will take its course. There's nothing we can do about that, just pray it ends up in your favor, I guess. Mom knew that and she accepted it. You should too. Just be happy with what you got," said Malcolm.

"Is that why you sell insurance?" Jordan asked his brother. "Car accidents, fires, suicides, people dying of cancer. I think you want to keep people from experiencing what you went through. It has a certain, what do you call it, fatalism to it. You want to help them."

"Elizabeth said that, too, tried to make a moral case for what I do. Honestly, it never crossed my mind. Just something I was good at that paid well," said Malcolm.

Jordan slugged back his beer, drowning in a thought. "Our family is cursed."

"Would you stop with that, sick of hearing it." Malcolm slammed his glass hard on the bar. "Life is a death sentence, that's the only curse. You know, you've been stuck on this since the moment we came home. Leah told me—"

"When did you see Leah?"

"Before I came here," Malcolm answered. "When I say I was
out looking for you, I wasn't lying. I was worried, so was she. How
long will it take to get it through your head that a real living breathing person, two of them, at least, care about what happens to
you?" Malcolm drank, exhausted. "I'm sick of having to do this
over and over. I am here to get married, God forbid have a little
bit of fun. Instead, I've chased you around half the Ozarks while
you piece together some theory that for all you know could be a
rather impressive creation of your own imagination. She said you
followed someone yesterday?"

"I swear I seen him before. Turns out I was right," Jordan said.
"Son of a bitch has been following me since I left Texas, you too.
This is what I have been trying to tell you, only I didn't know the
scope of it yet. They knew the moment you and Elizabeth left
Little Rock. They have our home addresses, photographs of me
and you, old ones of Dad and Jake. They know everything about
us. I had a feeling something was going on, like we were being followed everywhere we went—that night in the grove, at the casino.
So when I saw Cob—that's the little one's name—I followed him.
He does the bidding of this guy named Grieves. Must be a hundred
years old, taller than a tree. Real freak of nature."

Jordan dug into his pocket and spread out a folded-up bar
napkin. "When I followed Cob out to their cabin, this is what
I saw." He pointed at figures scrawled in his messy handwriting,
crudely drawn symbols, signs, and a sequence of numbers that
could possibly have been dates.

"Do you know what any of these mean?"

Jordan tossed the napkin over on the bar and shook his head.

Malcolm was more confused than before, but now believed that Jordan believed he was onto something. "I still don't know how any of that relates to us. What is it you think they want?"

"I think they're planning on killing Dad." Jordan sat back and threw up his hands. "Why? I have no idea."

Malcolm scoffed.

The bartender checked on them. Jordan waved him off.

"If you're so serious, then we should go to the police, let them deal with it," said Malcolm.

"Yeah, that's not going to happen."

"Why not?"

"Because those pig fuckers won't do a Goddamned thing but make everything worse and somehow I'll end up back in prison." Jordan sat, fuming. "You hear me? No cops."

"Okay, I get it. Pariah to authority, how could I forget," said Malcolm.

Jordan gulped down his beer and collected himself. "Besides," he said. "Even if we wanted to, we couldn't go to the cops." He scanned the filthy floor as he chose what was proving to be some delicate phrasing. "Andridge, the tall one," Jordan said quietly. "He's tied up in a room at the motel next door."

Malcolm wrapped a palm across his eyes, shaking his head. "Please tell me you're joking." He leaned off the stool toward his brother, growling. "Are you insane? You were the one who was just talking about prison. Are you that eager to go back? You're a convicted felon, Jordan." He exhaled in disbelief and rocked his weight back on the cheap vinyl cushion. "What were you planning on doing with him?" Malcolm's face sank as he thought the worst. "Wait, what have you done to him?"

Jordan finally landed his eyes on his brother and explained how he had only asked Andridge a few questions.

"Did he tell you anything?" Malcolm asked.

"Not much. The man speaks in riddles." Jordan trailed off, not wanting to proceed. "There was one thing, though." Malcolm made an impatient face. "All right, God. He said you were going to kill Dad."

"What the hell is that supposed to mean?"

"It's bullshit, I know."

"Did he say anything else?"

"That was it, I swear."

Without warning, Malcolm hooked Jordan rough under the arm and yanked him to his feet. "Let's go," he told him, tossing a crisp twenty on the bar.

"Come on, man." He shoved back Malcolm and straightened himself.

Malcolm gathered Jordan's coat that was spread across the seat of his stool and whipped it in his face. "I told you not to fuck with me," he said.

They kicked dirt through the parking lot as Jordan struggled to keep up with his brother. Dull light guided their way from bent posts. Solitary cars shot by in the opposite direction. They walked up the shoulder of the road to the motel, where two stories were split by a warped railing that wrapped around the inside of the court.

Jordan asked Malcolm what he was going to do. "I'm going to find out what kind of game this son of a bitch is playing. Then you are going to act like you are part of civil society for once in your miserable life and let him go. Then we are going to go back home. Tomorrow, I am going to get married, and we are going to pretend that none of this ever happened." Malcolm asked Jordan if he understood. Jordan nodded as he fumbled with the blue plastic triangle that swung from the key and opened the door to room sixteen.

The bed was made square under the jaundiced hue that dissipated from the lamp on the nightstand. A whiskey bottle, cups, and a deflated bag of chili chips sat on the table beside a legal pad filled with Jordan's writing and a plastic tray piled with miniature mountains of ash. The muted television danced with thousands of floating dead fish. The chair was angled between the television and the door, ripped strips of duct tape torn in every direction. The empty chair pinned the room together with one resounding truth—Andridge was gone.

Jordan rushed onto the balcony and searched the parking lot. Malcolm checked in the shower and behind the bathroom door, but knew this supposedly nefarious giant was nowhere to be found. Jordan came back in the room and watched the fish float and smoke rise from a fertilizer plant until Malcolm switched off the television. He dragged over the empty chair and dropped his weight in it. Malcolm unscrewed the cap on the whiskey bottle, righted two paper cups, and poured carefully until they were full. He reached one of the cups toward Jordan, shaking it a little to entice him.

"Come over here," he said. "Drink this."

FIFTEEN

The troubadours plucked mandolins and strummed parlor guitars, hoping to drive customers to their tents. Hand-painted signs advertised the latest cure-alls made from aromatic herbs, rhizomes of swamp grass, dried root bark, diuretics, and unknown amounts of morphine. Everyone recognized the town drunk as he stumbled through the carnival grounds. Sonny was a big man who staggered with a permanent slope in his back caused by a cracked vertebra. Rogue fragments of bone floated next to a ball of Union lead lodged close enough to his nervous cord that the field doctor at Wilson's Creek refused to go near it for fear of killing him right there on the gurney.

Sonny crashed through one of the tents, making a show of counting the coins in his hand, knowing they were not enough. He hoped one of the patent mediciners would take pity on him—a crippled hero of the Rebellion, vagrant split apart by tremors, he didn't care which condition did the trick as long as he got a drink. He only needed enough to stop the delirium, which he knew would be coming soon enough. The sides of his vision were already swirling in clouds of pearl. After that, he only had a few minutes to react before his sight fell into a hole and his memory along with it. Hopefully, he would find a safe corner where he could sleep it off instead of ending up in the stockade, where local jailers took turns beating him with knotted ropes and pissing in his face.

A vendor in a purple hat leaned through a fold in the canvas. "Lookin' mighty sick there, old boy. Come on in, I got what suits yah n' cures what ails yah." Sonny raised his gruff but soft voice enough to inquire about the cost of an elixir that promised to quell his aches and pains. "Can't do nothin' in that way for yah," said the raconteur. He scanned his wares and grabbed a small green bottle from the bottom of a nearby crate. "Try this here, a gift from me to you," he said, eyeing Sonny as he drank it. Sonny swallowed most the contents of the bottle in his first desperate swig, his face wretched, and he nearly folded himself in half as he spit up in the dirt. The vendor roared with laughter. "That there is the finest Indian tapeworm killer this side of paradise. Fit to put them Connecticut Kickapoo crooks right out the business!"

Sonny hobbled away, furious as he hacked the bitter burn from his throat. He'd not had a drink for hours, his skull ached, and the earth grew dim. He thought it best to get on while he still could and find a place to nap. He only needed to kill a few hours before meeting with his friend Andridge later that night. Sonny and Andridge had fought together in the war. They helped each other survive, even lay wounded side by side, and kept each other company while they healed and waited to be discharged. There was no one on this smoking earth that Sonny Bayne trusted more than Andridge Sampson.

His sons, Sherman and Abner Bayne, held court at the local tavern singing Irish ditties and soldiering hymns for nickels and free drinks. Business was best on holidays and when the fairs began. They sold their act on the fact that they were twins, not identical, of course, but they told people they were and made it work. *The Tawny Twins*, the bill read, *sing any song from Tralee to Tennessee. A nickel for one, a dime for three, a round of ale enthusiastically imbibed by we. Too-ra-loo, too-ra-lee, let us sing a song for thee!*

The brothers had bushy hair and wide, garrulous smiles. Their arms were round and heavy, muscles built after they took over the family farm from their father. In the years following the war, Sonny could not bear physical labor due to his injuries and the land fell into disrepair. Andridge had sent over two black farmhands to assist, but the soil had gone to seed and the crops suffered one ailment after another, burning in summer droughts and dying beneath drifts of winter snow. The boys heaved dead crops out of the ground and replanted new ones. They hoped the rows would spring to life each new year, but it never took, as though the land itself had shut down. When Sherman and Abner came of age, the land too slowly came back to life. They drove the wedge plow and cut the field back to the timber line and together walked the rows with their hobbled father as he explained the cycle of the harvest.

The tavern rang with jubilant cheers as Sherman and Abner finished their last song and toasted their mugs in celebration. Sherman let out a yell, then laid a sloppy kiss on Margerie, the black-haired maven he was promised to marry. She anchored an arm around Sherman and the other around Abner, who tensed the muscles in his neck and smiled sheepishly as she swung her tight body between them.

"Y'all see that Crescent Hotel fixing to open in Eureka Springs?" Margerie asked. "My, does it look luxurious! We should go this summer. It's been so hot, they got them health baths with that good water. Wouldn't that be just fine? You could save up here. Between that and harvest, I reckon we could afford it. How about it, Sherman. Want to take me?"

"I sure like the idea of you bathing all right," he said. "Don't know how you plan on getting down there, though. Those railroad boys are refusing to work again."

"I thought that was only Missouri," she said.

"From what I hear it's the whole MKT line, any track that some bitch Gould owns. The lines that ain't shut down been targeted for attack. Tracks been heaped with rocks and hammered to hell. Yesterday I read they done blowed up the Pine Bluff switch house."

Sherman swigged his mug and laughed from his belly. Margerie turned her attention to Abner, pressing her chest against the broad of his back. "Abe will take me—won't you, Abe?"

Abner gazed into his beer, embarrassed by her flirtation, angry that his brother's insistence on calling him Abe had spread to Margerie. When they were young, other boys hurled taunts at him, like *Abe, Abe, he love them slaves*, labeling him a turncoat for bearing the namesake of Lincoln. Abner was big and slow and easy to pick on, but when Sherman stood at his brother's side they were near impossible to beat in a fight. Abner begrudged accepting his brother's help, knowing full well that it came with the price of Sherman tormenting him whenever he wanted. Abner grew to size and beat half the schoolyard, with his brother's help, and eventually they stopped regarding him as easy prey. Taunts and name-calling faded until no one called him Abe anymore. No one except Sherman.

He charged outside and basked in night air far cooler than the humid tavern. He lit half a cigar, leaned against the outside of the pub, and closed his eyes.

"Kind of night that makes blood boil," a soft voice said.

Abner opened his eyes to see their family friend Andridge approaching him in the alley. "Hey there, Mr. Sampson. Boy, you just appeared out of nowhere."

"How else does someone appear?"

The entire time Abner had known him, Andridge Sampson was preoccupied with truths, both evident and hidden, but Abner thought he merely spoke about commonplace things in a round-about way. His father called him the local philosopher.

"Speaking of boiling blood," said Abner, leering through the window. "I'm sick of my brother needling me all the time," he said. "I ain't too trustful of his girl Margerie, neither. Since she come around he's been meaner than ever. I wish she would just go away, but he's probably going to marry her. To be honest with you, Mr. Sampson, I can't stand the thought of her bein' family."

Andridge lit himself a pipe and glanced down the alley at the crowded street, then motioned for Abner to listen close. "What if I was to make you privy to a rarified bit of information that could help you with your little problem?" he proposed.

In consideration, Abner never wanted to see Margerie again, and he wanted his old brother back, but he also did not want to cause any trouble. If anything were to happen, he could not bear being the cause of it. "All right, Mr. Sampson," he said, reticent. "What do you know?"

"Cute little Margerie in there has been laying with your father. She and Sonny been at it for the last two months, if I may be sure." Andridge watched the hope drain from Abner's eyes as he fell be-hind the murky gray cloud, speechless.

Andridge had another secret, one he would not dare speak or let see the light of day. He lusted after young Margerie, too, and wished for nothing more than to confess his love to her. Being a man of cunning and intelligence, Andridge hatched a plan that would kill two birds with one stone, as the saying goes. He had known the twins since birth and was acutely aware of Sherman's propensity for anger. Abner, plain as he was, would tell his brother about his fiancée's infidelity and Sherman would confront his father in a drunken rage, removing him from the equation, while simultaneously ending their relationship. With Sherman and Sonny out of the way, Andridge would have a clear path to Margerie's crooked heart.

Abner waited until later that night to tell Sherman the terrible news. Margerie had left soon after he went back inside, so he got incredibly drunk with his brother and sang one late-night round, doing everything he could to suppress the expansive sadness swelling within. He had thought poorly of his brother's betrothal to Margerie, but learning he was right to have suspected her only felt worse and he condemned himself for ever thinking such an awful thought. He wished he never mentioned anything about it to begin with. He suffered the impression that his harping, negative castigations had somehow assisted her betrayal and brought it into their lives. Though it had nothing to do with him, Abner languished under the guilt until he could take it no more.

Drunkard shapes faded into languorous chatter and the humid weather of the barroom. Abner crossed his forearms on the bar and looked over at his brother, whose forehead snapped down then rose back up, eyes half shut. There was no easy recourse, so Abner said it out loud just as Andridge had, more or less out of nowhere. A geyser of anger rushed through Sherman. Previously limber, he grew stiff with rage and swiped his beer clear off the counter as the last drunks in the barroom cheered. He gripped the sides of his face until hatred boiled through his eyes, then helped himself to his feet on his brother's broad shoulder.

"Where is he," he mumbled. "Where is our father?"

Abner had no answer and turned away as Sherman's fist smashed into his cheek. "Tell me now or I swear I'll do it again," he slurred.

Abner knew his brother would hit him ten more times if that was what it took, so he told him that he had heard they left the fair together. He agonized over the implications of what he was about to say, then admitted there was a possibility that they were back at the house. Sherman charged through the last of the crowd out of the tavern, beating the dirt of the thoroughfare through a gauntlet of straw torches.

The beautiful White Lillie removed the last of her targets from the shooting gallery. The fire eater soaked his iron rods in a steaming vat. Comics flipped cards with the girls from the peep show and the ominous fakirs, dry-skinned and road-weary, leant a hand loading ponies and prairie dogs into stacks of wire cages. Abner chased Sherman among the attractions and the cluttered alleyways that let out behind the tents. After a brief pursuit, he realized he had lost him. Abner paced around, frantic, until he was able to garner a horse from a local stable owner on the promise that he return it by morning or pay double the rate.

He rode up to the house and found his brother's horse tied up out front. The coarse, drunken throes of Sherman's voice carried inside the house, and Abner ran in but stopped outside the bedroom, deflated by his realization that there was nothing to be done. His brother had always been in command and his anger had no equal. Even if he wanted to intervene, he knew in his heart that when the time came he would do nothing more than shrink in quietude and make sure he stayed out of the way, just as he always did.

Sonny and Margerie were bare in bed, heads propped against the dasher as they cowered back from Sherman towering in the doorway. His father held out his arms, begging Sherman to come to his senses.

"How could you do this to me?" he asked. "You are my father, my flesh and blood."

"I am weak, son. The booze got me. I don't even know why I do the things I do anymore. I am sorry, you have to forgive me, please—"

"Shut up. I am sick of hearing about weakness. Weak this, weak that, this world ain't for no weak," he yelled.

Margerie covered herself with the sheet, but reasoned it was nothing both of them had not seen, so she let the white fabric fall from the flesh of her nipples, revealing her chest.

Sherman turned his attention to her. "You just go around to anyone that will have you now, that it?" He shook in a crying, maniacal fit. "I loved you, Margerie. Truly, I did."

Margerie erupted with laughter. "Could you be more pathetic? I would have had to put all three of you Baynes together to get one real man." She rose naked from the bed and began to slip her legs through her undergarments.

Abner peeked inside the doorway, stared at Margerie's breasts, down her lean stomach to her black tuft, then looked away. When she tried to step past Sherman to reach for her blouse, he pulled her by her arm and punched her in the back of the head. Sonny struggled out of bed but Sherman kicked him back down and threw Margerie on top of him. Ravenous, Sherman scanned the room until he fixed on the kerosene lamp flickering on the dresser. He picked it up, the base full of yellow viscous. He sloshed the fuel back and forth and raised the lamp, casting its light toward the bed.

"You two will lay together for the rest of eternity," he said, calm and distant as he threw the lamp across the room. Margerie screamed and Sherman watched as his father wrapped his arms around her. Glass smashed on the wall above their heads and a ball of fire exploded in a brilliant flash of light. The flaming oil leapt along the wall and rained down on Margerie and Sonny. They scrambled flaming from the bed, but Sherman kicked them back down and stood over them until their screams softened and the roar of the fire took hold. The two bodies twisted and flailed, skin burned white to red, bodies charred to black, until the corpses condensed into an indiscernible ball of flesh.

The fire quickly spread from the bodies to the burning bed and climbed up the ceiling with frightening speed. Surrounding air was sucked into the fire, daring Abner to draw one last scalding breath as he ran into the room and dragged his brother out. Sherman did not resist. He fell catatonic as Abner hugged him around the chest and dragged him out the front door of the smoke-filled house and laid him in the grass.

From the yard, Abner watched the back of the house seep out waves of white smoke before it was eaten by the roaring flames. Sherman had got to his feet and staggered toward the woods by the roadside. Abner went after him but stopped when he heard a horse galloping over the hill and saw Andridge Sampson emerge from the dark, entranced by the spectacle of fire. The house calved apart under spires of flame. Andridge rode up as close as he could get and came to a stop, cradled in his saddle.

"They're both dead," Abner called from his seat on the lawn. Two little fires grew in the tears on Andridge's face. The burning house claimed the man to whom he owed his life and Margerie, his unrequited love. Their ashes floated from the burning house onto the mane of Andridge's horse, his shoulders, and the brim of his hat, covering them like fallen snow.

SIXTEEN

DOWNTOWN JASPER MOVED SLOW, the way plants grow. Shop windows were clouded with circular swaths of dried water and the faded awnings of shops hung brittle and listless in the early morning. Walker parked his beat-up truck in a row of empty spots angled in front of Eberle's feed store, where his oldest friend Rubin Bodine walked to the edge of the clapboard porch and leaned against a post, fatigued.

"Coming from church?" Walker asked him.

"Mhm," Rubin grumbled. "I's late, too. Stopped on the way to pick a dead dog out the road. She was a mutt with no tags, awful skinny, must have been out there a while. Reminded me of Lester, sweet boy. That's just me, taking pity on any old suffering thing."

"He ain't suffering no more," said Walker. "What'd you do with her?"

"Laid her in the back and brought her to the vet to be disposed of proper," he said.

"Hell of a way to spend a morning," said Walker.

"Pickin' up feed for the new hogs." Rubin nodded toward the store and Walker offered to give him a hand.

As long as Walker had known Rubin, he had an affinity for pigs and kept a stable of them at his house. His father raised them and Rubin grew affection for them at a young age. When he was in his twenties he brought a newborn piglet named Arnold on their tour bus for thirty shows in forty nights. He never failed to remind the boys that by the end of that trip Arnold smelled better than any of them did. Rubin lost six full-grown hogs last winter. Two fell from intestinal rot, four contracted pneumonia—hog cough, as Rubin called it—and died by month's end. Rubin could not afford to treat them, underwater as he was on account of his own health troubles. He blamed himself not paying them enough care. When the cold let up for a brief spell last January, the ground thawed enough for Walker to head over to the farm and help Rubin bury his oldest. The mound was still there behind the pen. They hauled away the rest in the same truck bed they now tossed a dozen bags of feed into, pausing to rest from the strain.

"Jury's in," Walker said between wheezes. "If there's such a thing as too old, we're it."

"Ain't no such nothin'. We turning over, that's all." Rubin took his time back and forth out of the store, finally lifting the last bag of grain over the lip of the tailgate. "Not much else for us to do but keep something else alive," he said, patting the bag of grain.

"Watch your kid get married," Walker added.

Rubin wiped the sweat from his brow with a balled handkerchief, nodding in agreement.

"I'm buying up what ice they got over there at the grocery, now you hop in with me and return the favor," said Walker.

Rubin hacked up a brutal cough that doubled him over at the knees. Over the years, Walker learned to respect Rubin's pride by not extending a hand to console him or even ask about his welfare. He just stared down Main Street until he was finished. Rubin cleared his lungs and said, "The worse I feel, the lighter my burden gets."

Malcolm sat on the edge of his childhood bed twirling a flower he'd plucked from one of the bouquets on the table downstairs before Mary shoved him away. "Elizabeth's going to come down any minute," she informed him. "You get gone." He managed a moment alone upstairs when Harrell poked his head through the open door.

"There you are," he said. "Listen, before I forget, Russ wanted me to tell you how sorry he was for things getting out of hand the other night."

Malcolm told him Russ had no need to worry.

"Well, he's shook up about it. Combine that with drinking and his love of pills and you've got two different people. He really is a good guy, just been through a lot. He's been in freefall since his brother died. I try to be there for him when it hits, but it knocks him near into another dimension. Up is down, black is white—"

"Rape is all right," Malcolm interrupted. "That is what you are saying, isn't it?"

"Fuck no, he deserves what's coming to him," Harrell said. "I ain't one to keep defending him. Like I said, it gets tiresome."

"Waitresses everywhere will rejoice," said Malcolm. He could tell Harrell was uncomfortable. "At some point it's not your problem. You're being a good friend and all, but I have been back here, what, a week? He jumped me in the parking lot outside the bar and who knows what he would have done to that girl if I hadn't happened to hear her scream. You say it's a matter of time. The time is here, Harrell."

The silence was shattered when a caterer dropped a stack of chafing trays down the stairs. Malcolm shot to his feet and stormed out to the landing. "What are you doing?" he asked.

"I'm sorry," she said, startled. "I thought these were supposed to go up here," the girl said.

"What makes you think they go up here? The wedding is out-side." Malcolm held out his arms and looked around, incredulous. "Outside," he yelled. Harrell helped her pick up the trays as they both went back down the stairs.

Though it was early afternoon, the house had already filled with guests and more continued to arrive. Jordan careened through the front of the house, working on his third day drunk. He made a commotion bumping into an end table, knocking over a ceramic clock. Elizabeth broke from a group of her relatives and hurried over to pick the clock up off the floor. "Not a scratch," she said, examining it for damages. "Would you look at that." Elizabeth looked around, then forced Jordan's limber weight to a corner in the living room. "Where in the world have you been? Malcolm was worried, all of us were."

"I don't like it when people worry about me." He did his best to dismiss her concern. "Plus, I'm not about to upset the bride on her wedding day."

"You better not be." Elizabeth forced a nervous smile, then pulled him close. "Listen to me, take a deep breath. You are around people who love you. There ain't nothing to be afraid of here. We are here to celebrate love, to celebrate family." Jordan tried to pull away but Elizabeth tightened her grip on the back of his neck. "So sober up and go get dressed."

Jordan's head pounded, his brain sopped with alcohol. He cinched an eye closed and the room came into focus. The house was lined from wall to wall with acquaintances, friends of the fam-ily and their children, and people he did not recognize. He walked through the crowd, slowly progressing toward the kitchen. Hands reached for his shoulder and slapped him on the back. Voices leapt out in recognition, calling him by name. Faces solidified and memory began to fill in the gaps. An old bandmate of Walker's stopped Jordan in his tracks.

"Jordan, it's Jim Cleary," he said jovially. "I haven't seen you since you since you were yea tall." He gestured with his hand beside his waist.

It took a moment for Jordan to recognize him from the photograph in the downstairs hall. "I know you. You played music with my father."

"From the sound of it, it's you who's making the music nowadays. Your father couldn't be more proud, but I'm sure you hear that all the time. It was good seeing you, Jordan. Enjoy the ceremony."

Jordan walked past him with a furrowed brow. He stepped around Elizabeth's aunts, Ashley and Mary, as they wrangled together a group of fidgeting children for a picture. He recognized Malcolm's old boss, Ben Ringgold, talking to his wife by the island in the kitchen, where he poured black coffee from a carafe and downed the cup in a mouthful before refilling it. Harrell came up beside him, speaking in a hushed tone. "My parents are right behind you, be cool."

"We are so delighted for your brother," said Harrell's mother, embracing Jordan.

He reciprocated the stern handshake of Harrell's father, who thanked Jordan for having invited them

"Don't thank me," Jordan said.

"He means your whole family," she corrected her husband. "Y'all must have worked so hard to put all this together. Rest assured, the big day is finally here."

Harrell kissed his mother on the cheek and promised he would catch up with them before the ceremony. Harrell and Jordan joined Baron and Johnny outside on the deck. Johnny was already smoking and handed Jordan one from his pack, lighting it. Jordan exhaled smoke with the air still stuck in his lungs from inside. "That was strange," he said to Harrell. "I thought your parents hated me."

"What are you talking about? My parents love you. Couldn't tell you why, but they do."

"Enough of that," Baron interrupted. "What happened to you after the bachelor party? I heard you disappeared."

"Something I had to take care of. Everything is fine now."

"You mean *someone*." Johnny blew smoke down his beard, looking around at the guys. "You know he's back with Leah, right?"

They exploded in a commotion, pushing and shoving Jordan with cajoling congratulations. Jordan warded them off. "Maybe the next wedding will be yours," said Harrell.

"We'll see if we make it through today," Jordan countered.

The boys were already working on their buzz and argued over which bridesmaids they had eyes on. Jordan retreated to examine an unfamiliar welling of relief. When he realized that he was the only one responsible for keeping this rising feeling of peace from taking hold, he resigned and let it spread to everything around him. If he didn't know any better, Jordan guessed this was what home felt like.

Josh Bodine hopped up the porch steps by twos, looking frazzled. "Here's the deal," he told Jordan. "We've got too much music gear and too little time to load it. I was hoping you could give us a hand?"

"Sure thing."

Behind a closet door hung with garments, Elizabeth inspected her delicate skin, the way it wrapped around the thin curves of her exposed collar bones. She pinned up the last of her hair and covered her chest as her mother came in dangling a white silk slip from a hanger. They were using Walker's bedroom as the bridal quarter. There was enough space, an attached bathroom, and most importantly, it sat at the far end of the upstairs hallway, away from the steady bustle enveloping the rest of the house.

Mary was struck by the beauty of her daughter laid bare. She knew she was a grown woman, but she saw her daughter at all ages across all times in the portent of youth that glowed in her bright expression. She could see through time, back to the nubile skin of her baby, to her birth, and before, when Elizabeth was nothing more than an unformed vessel, a yearning, an idea. That child looked back at her now, never having been diminished, only added to and built upon. The tears were quick to Mary's eyes as she kissed her daughter's forehead.

"Mom, you can't start that already. Get it out now. Once I do my makeup, you are forbidden from crying," Elizabeth warned her.

She cleared the wavering pools from the bottoms of her eyes and handed over the slip, which Elizabeth hung beside her dress on the back of the door. Mary caressed the pattern on the crest of the hem and thought it felt like crushed flowers. When Elizabeth came out in the slip, Mary lined up behind her in the mirror, held her around the waist, and kissed the back of her neck. "This is going to be so good for you two," she said. "You have been doing so well, working so hard, this makes it all worth it. I know its cliché, but really it will," Mary said.

Elizabeth looked at her mother behind her in the mirror and asked if that was what marrying her father did for her.

"My marriage to your father, short as it was, turned out to be the happiest time of my life. We had you, pure joy shining on both our lives. It was like the universe gave all the happiness we could ever wish for right back to us. I have no complaints, dear."

"It can turn so quick though, can't it?" Elizabeth asked.

"We don't need to talk about that. I am happier than I have ever been, I'm about to watch my sweet daughter get married. This should be one of the happiest days of your life," she said. "Happiness doesn't just come, you have to work for it." She brushed her daughter's hair back. "You have earned this, Lizzie. Remember to enjoy it."

"Funny you say that, Mom. Turns out I have a lot to be grateful for." Elizabeth hovered her hand around the slender paunch of her stomach and they glanced at it together in the mirror. "I'm pregnant," Elizabeth whispered, crushed by tears.

"Oh, honey," Mary cried. She squeezed Elizabeth and barraged the side of her face with kisses, sobbing.

"Malcolm doesn't know. I've been waiting for the right time to tell him."

"No time like the present," she said. "He'll be so happy."

Elizabeth's aunts crashed into the room pouring champagne over a handful of crystal glasses.

"You girls have good timing." Mary looked at her daughter intently. "Elizabeth's expecting," she announced.

A chorus of high-pitched screams enveloped the room as the women surrounded her with one big hug. "Malcolm doesn't know?" they asked.

"It has all gone by so fast," she said. "I was going to tell him tonight."

"You already got him on the hook to marry you, hun. What can he say?" Margaret was boisterous and already a little buzzed.

"You are terrible," Mary told her.

"What?" she replied. "It does unexpected things to them. My Randy was petrified at first. He grew up an only child. Even though he was a grown man, he went right back to that, as though it formed the basis for how he was going to be a parent. It brings up a whole lot you don't expect, that's all I am saying."

"Why do you have to be so contrary?" Mary asked, defensive. "Give me that," she said, taking the bottle of Jouet away from her and refilling her and Elizabeth's glasses. "Here you go, sweetie. Don't pay any mind to the lamentations of the old and depressed." Mary fell back in a chair, crossed her legs, and swigged her champagne, unable to shake the enamored look from her face. "See what you have to look forward to?"

A worn Martin D-28 and a Sterling banjo with a signature scrawled on the drum hung from hooks above Malcolm's head. He reclined in one of two leather smoking chairs in blue boxers and an unbuttoned collared shirt. Walker inched forward in the other chair, handed his son a crystal tumbler of Colonel Taylor, then leaned back and sipped from his own. "This wedding brought us back together," Walker told him. "Elizabeth is just a doll. Mary and Ashley have been a pleasure to have around these past few days as well. You did good, son."

"Ah, I see." Malcolm laughed and nudged his father. "You just like having women around."

Walker twirled the amber liquid in the deep of his glass. "Maybe so," he said. "It has been a long time, hasn't it."

"Why didn't you remarry?" Malcolm asked in earnest.

"I meant to. Never got around to it, I suppose."

Malcolm inhaled the burn of the whiskey. "For once in your life, give me the real reason, please. I want to know."

"It's not like that," said Walker. "Time gets away from you, is all. It's elusive, the more you go after it the more it pulls away, and the more it takes with it. After your mother died, I panicked. I didn't know the first thing about raising you boys. Mercy was a saint, in that regard. She had the sense women have to create a home, make a place proper. I ain't come from that. When she passed, my heart broke. Not only did raising you and Jordan become my responsibility, it became my way of coping. I did my best to move on, but if I'm being honest, I don't know that I ever did. Only later I learned that I may not have dealt with your mother's death in the right way. I never rebuilt a home for either of you, and before I knew it, I turned around and this place was abandoned. You were working full time at fifteen, like I did when I was your age. I wasn't going to stop you. Your brother was already a handful of hell by then, there was nothing I could do. It was too late. Everything was already set on its course. It took a lot of years sitting here alone for me to realize what I done. I ain't proud of it, but it was all I could do to get through."

He stared into his glass, gathering himself. "But that's not going to happen to you. You and Elizabeth got your whole lives before you, and I'm just so proud."

"Like you said, we're back here now, after all this time. For a celebration, no less. Maybe it did turn out okay," Malcolm assured his father.

"Maybe you're right."

Malcolm cleaned up and put on his suit. Guests milled around the porch and the driveway, filing into the backyard. Well-dressed couples, single bachelors, elder widows, and spritely children poured into the house. They shook hands and hugged as waiters ticketed jackets and brought drinks. The dull thud of music could be heard through the basement walls.

Jordan pushed his way into the music room with Malcolm's groom party, their eyelids slack and ties loosed. Harrell pulled the cork from a bottle with his teeth and produced a handful of Habano cigars. After an hour, Mary came downstairs and announced that the bride was ready. Malcolm straightened his tie one last time, then went over to Jordan and straightened his disheveled vest. They lined up in the corridor and waited in front of the basement door. Malcolm led them out, and it was only when he took his first step onto the gravel that he noticed it had been raining for quite some time.

SEVENTEEN

Rain fell on Elizabeth as she proceeded to the altar in flowing white. Malcolm stood under the awning watching his bride approach on a wetted tract of emerald. She reached the step and he took her hand. The small crowd quieted when Herbert Reed, the elder pastor from Walker's church, raised his hand and began the ceremony. He thanked young and old, family and friend for gathering as witness to the union of Malcolm Bayne and Elizabeth May Truitt. He joked that he was sure the rain was a sign of fertility and growth. Seated in the front row, Mary forced a knowing look with her daughter.

Elizabeth took in the faces gathered under a scaffold of rolling clouds and immersed herself in a rightness of place. Then she looked to the skinny, confident boy she had met one afternoon on her way to the campus library, standing now at her side, ready to stand there for life. Malcolm's was a secret language she had learned to speak. She had been an open book for most of her life, a trait that first gained Malcolm's interest and later his love. The closer they became the more he felt his love returned in ways he never could have fathomed. Malcolm came from people who wore themselves like leather, hearts guarded to withstand the next catastrophe. The surety of disaster lodged itself in his blood. No matter how safe, happy, or fulfilled, Malcolm was descended from a line for whom, more often than not, the worst tended to occur. Elizabeth had undone some of that hardwiring of inherent distrust. She softened his indifference, broke down his inner defenses, and he let himself turn into a person he actually wanted to become.

A nurturing, challenging embrace that led them there, held in the breadth of hills and the river, to be married on land that Malcolm's ancestors had fought to keep, whose every decision to persist in sparse times led directly to Malcolm's life and the introduction of love into her own. Elizabeth felt a swell of gratitude, thankful for the persistence and continued renewal of the land itself. This deep appreciation formed the foundation of her vows, which she began to speak.

The ring was a thin gold band with a small stone at the center, which, after completing his repetition of the same vows, Malcolm slid onto Elizabeth's trembling finger, then she did the same for him. Pastor Reed raised the timbre of his voice, orating to the crowd. "By the power vested in me by the State of Arkansas, and the Church of our lord and savior, Jesus Christ, I now pronounce you husband and wife. You may kiss the bride." Malcolm pulled Elizabeth closed and kissed her, sensual and slow, to a rising tide of cheers. They clasped each other's hands and raised them overhead, then walked together through the applauding crowd. Many festivities had taken place on Bayne land—birthdays, reunions, holidays, concerts, parties, and auctions—but never had there been a wedding, until today.

Children ran in small suits and dresses, soaked from the rain and sliding in the mud. The house filled up with those looking to get warm and dry. Mary assisted Walker in fixing hot water for tea as the caterers carried out trays of shrimp and cheddar grits, hushpuppies, and stuffed mushrooms. The bar outside was crushed by a line of eager drinkers. Ladies carried full armloads of white wines and vodka tonics back to smaller groups. Men talked and stood to the side holding beers.

Stunning in a robin's egg dress, Leah Fayette brought Jordan a beer and kissed his newly shaved face. "I brought my friend, Marissa," she said. "Hope that's fine. You met her the first night you were back. She was so embarrassed by that." Jordan waved and Marissa offered a head nod in return. "Looks like Harrell's already hitting on her pretty hard." Leah laughed.

"I can get him to leave her alone if you like," Jordan offered.

"Nah, it's good for her, Harrell's nice enough," she said. "So, how are you feeling? Did all that turn out okay? You know your brother came looking for you."

Jordan lit a smoke. "Suppose I never will learn the truth about the whole thing," he said. "Don't feel crazy no more, though. Ain't in some things' nature to be known, I guess." He finished his drink and stared off.

Leah wrapped both arms around his sides. "All you need to know is how fond I am of this man standing before me," she said, pulling him close.

A pang of feedback rang from the stage, followed by the clean thumbing of a blues chord. Rubin Bodine plugged in a beat-up Gretsch and took the stage with his band of old-timers, sons and grandchildren, which he introduced as the Moon Falls String Band. They settled into a slow tune that got hips swaying and saw Malcolm lead Elizabeth onto the floor for their first dance. When the fiddler picked it up, etching an energetic melody that quickened the tempo, Walker stepped in and took Elizabeth's hand. Malcolm swayed to the edge of the parquet panels sopping with rain and grabbed Mary Truitt by the waist and swung her among the dancing crowd. The warmth of celebration and drunkenness propelled dancers across the floor. Wicker torches reflected in pools of water floating with blades of grass. The stage was lit by a single floodlight, the beam cut by sideways rain.

Rubin sat at the front of the stage with his semi-hollow heaped in his lap and cleared his throat into the microphone. "I would like you all to raise a glass to the beautiful bride, and the considerably less attractive groom." The crowd cheered with laughter. "I known this boy here since before he could walk, so I can rib him like that, see. It's all part of the blessing." Rubin squinted through the lights and rain, eventually finding Malcolm and Elizabeth in the crowd. "I had the good fortune to play music with your father some forty-five years ago. Can you believe? We were on top of the world then, made some great music together. Didn't we, Walker?" He searched the crowd until he found his old friend. Walker nodded his beard, flush with longing and joy. Rubin returned to Malcolm. "I knew your mother before she passed." His solitary address echoed through the speakers. "She was as beautiful spirit as there ever was. I seen her bring so much joy each day to your father and you boys when you was little. She gone that better way, but she would have been so proud here today. I can feel her, smiling down. You boys took after her, talk about blessed. Jordan looks a bit more like her. That's all right, Malcolm. That just means you are cursed to turn out like your father, wrinkled as a hide."

Clapping and hollering corralled the front of the stage and Rubin called on Walker to get up there and join him in playing a song. "Let's do a song for the new couple, Walker, and a few more for the rest of these freeloaders." At the prodding of friends and the Truitt women, Walker obliged Rubin's request and made his way to the stage. "Well, would you look at that," Rubin called over the clapping and yelling of the crowd. "Now, where's Jordan?"

Rubin scanned the crowd until he found him. "How's about playing one with your old man, son?" Jordan waved him off, but Leah
pushed him by the shoulders and parted the crowd.

Jordan smiled at his father and joined his side under the bright
light. Rubin got a lick rambling and cued the boys in the band to
follow suit. Rubin came back to the front and faced the crowd.
Jordan yelled in his ear, "What song are we doing?"

"An old one of your pa's, called 'Sanctimony.' Just sit backup
to the first chorus and you'll figure it out."

"I know it," Jordan said simply.

Malcolm swayed with his arms around Elizabeth and listened
to his father's ethereal voice as it was backed by his brother's natural harmony. They finished the tune to a thunder of applause and
the dancing couples called out for another.

"No, no," Walker grumbled through the speakers. He leaned
off to the side and told Rubin and Jordan that he was not feeling
well. "I'm awfully tired from an eventful couple of days," he said.
"Tell you what. I am going take a break for just a little while—
when I come back, we'll sing a few."

"That's a deal," said Rubin. Walker and Jordan embraced before Rubin helped him to the stairs at the side of the stage.

"I guess I'll play a few more then," said Jordan. Rubin slung his
guitar over his head and handed it over to Jordan. He threw the
leather strap over his shoulder and looked out on the people in
the drizzling night. He planted himself in front of the microphone
and steadily strummed, heat breaking in his chest, unknown weight
falling away. Leah watched from the foot of the stage and listened
to his coarse divination rumble atop his twanging guitar and roll
across the yard. Walker looked on for a moment, immersed in
an utter dispensation of peace. He had grown tired and heaved
his way through congratulatory guests, who shook his hand and

patted his shoulder as he passed. Jordan watched his father break free from the crowd and take his time crossing the grass up to the house, alone.

As Walker undressed in his room, the cacophony of the party was reduced to a murmur. He shed the exhaustion of incessant talking and constant socializing and reveled in the momentary quiet of the upstairs. The fast pace of the wedding had caught up with him, as well as an unexpected torrent of emotional relief. He hung his suit in the mahogany wardrobe anchored in the far corner of his bedroom and sat on the edge of his bed, removing his cuffs, watch, and rings, placing them on the nightstand. He switched off the bedside lamp and drifted to sleep.

Soft light glared through the fog blanketing an unfamiliar field. Walker stepped lightly on stiff stalks of grass and wild brush. Frosted straw brushed the sides of his legs. His breath melded into the haze. Cold and confused, he kept walking, each step heavy and slow. He did not know where he was or how he got there. The feeling of being followed burned at his back and he looked around, uneasy. He strained to see behind him, but there were only hazy flows of mist trapped by dark forest. He knelt in the grass to get a handle on his nerves, closing his eyes and steadying his breath. A quick, ephemeral sound cut the air ahead of him like wind once more before it disappeared.

His heart pounded on the back of his tongue and struggled to siphon blood to the tips of his numb extremities. He felt like a sitting duck, so he shot up and broke into a dead run, straw and horseweed whisked like insects as he charged past. He turned to look behind him, and a slow terror pulled his mouth apart. A shadowy figure was running after him through the fog. Walker quickened his pace, his only motivation to make it out of the open field and back into the cover of the trees. The remaining distance of the grove took a distorted amount of time and effort to dissipate and Walker feared that he wasn't going to make it out. The light that illuminated the field began to fade beneath the canopy that lay just ahead. Weakness fought to get a hold in his chest and the pain that rang through his legs pinched in his joints and knifed his body with white heat as he stumbled over uneven depressions that opened in the ground. Walker bounded over patches of mud and dead wood felled on its side. His speed decreased and the beast came closer. A root that was twisted above the ground caught Walker's foot and sent him crashing upon wet leaves and fallen branches.

He laid still, swallowing small, wheezing breaths. He gazed at the understory. The forest cracked and dripped, hidden nocturnal creatures howled and shrieked. He screwed his eyes closed again and huddled his knees to his chest in fear, like a child. The air sagged with the heat of another body, he could taste the residue of salt. He knew the creature was standing over him. The adrenaline that fueled his flight had waned and left in its hollow a pleading, defenseless, all-consuming dread. There was nothing left to do but face the unknown beast.

A muscular body rose out of the night covered in white ash, chest scored with symbols and scars. Circles divided by two lines dissected his stomach and abdomen. Walker scurried on his hands and knees back through dirt and leaves, petrified as the creature covered the ground that separated them with one giant step. Resolved upon the stratagem of its kill, the figure produced a blade. It hoisted the knife high in the night sky and a flash pierced the innermost chambers of Walker's heart. In that moment, Walker saw into the heart of the man who stalked and breathed like a monster. The shape of his body and the language of his sleek, lethal movement had felt eerily familiar, but it was not until the raising of the blade that the killer's face was laid bare. In the scoria of his eyes and the tough, blank canvas of his expression, Walker recoiled with horror as he deciphered the unmistakable face of his son.

Bluegrass rolled over dancing, writhing bodies. Elizabeth wrapped Malcolm's maroon sweatshirt over her dress to protect it from the rain, though the white hem was already soaked with muddy water. The interlocking floor panels bowed under stomping feet, slick with a film of rain, mud, grass, sweat, and spilled drinks. The gyrating mass of smiling dancers huddled together so they wouldn't slip and fall. Mary and Ashley Truitt danced in a group around Elizabeth while she kissed her new husband and swung her weight back and forth from his neck. "We did this, you and me," she said. "We brought all these people together. You should be proud. You know, you have another reason to be proud." Elizabeth began to mist with tears and grabbed Malcolm by the chin to be sure that she had his undivided attention. "You are going to be a father," she told him.

Malcolm's face froze with surprise. Then he kissed Elizabeth hard, dipping her down in a hug until they fell over together. He helped her to her feet as she oscillated between crying and hysterical laughter. "Dance with me," she pleaded, lacing his sky-blue tie through her fingers, rocking them close. Mary handed them both a fresh glass of wine, which they clanked together and sipped. Then Malcolm stepped on a slick floor panel and slid off balance, spilling the glass of cabernet down the front of his suit. He held out his glass, shirt and hand stained red.

Elizabeth laughed. "Don't you worry about that," she said, "just dance with me." She urged him closer, but Malcolm pulled back. "You're no fun," she said, directing his eyes to hers as she held her palm to his cheek. "Hey, look at me. It's a bit of spilled wine at a wedding, our wedding, in case you forgot." Malcolm calmed himself down. "Go get yourself cleaned up, a toothbrush and a little baking soda should do the trick," she instructed. "When you're done, you better get your ass back down here and dance with me."

Jordan let loose on Rubin's Gretsch, but as the evening wore on damp set in his bones, his fingers strickened with the cold, and he could think of nothing else but his conversation with Andridge Grieves and his insistence that Walker's life was somehow in danger. He worried where Andridge had gone after he disappeared from the hotel. He could not have taken kindly to Jordan's brief kidnapping and could be off somewhere plotting his revenge. He or Cob could be there right now, watching them. Though Jordan was worried about his father, he promised Malcolm that he would leave it alone, at least until after the wedding. He did what he could to put it out of his head, but it kept roaring back. He was not even sure what was in danger of happening, he only knew they were involved in something that was out of his control. All that speculative, horrid thinking was beginning to take its toll.

As he continued to play, he asked himself whether or not he really could have imagined the entire ordeal. If that were true, he was far more troubled by the prospect that he was losing his mind.

Walker returned from the depths of his dream scoured with sweat. He wiped threads of gray hair from his face, wildly eyeing the room. The bathroom door sat opened a crack. The dresser topped with pictures and a vase lamp stood heavy in the corner. A mahogany mirror reflected the far side of the room, where two red orbs with diamonds cut out of them hovered past the end of the bed. White chalk textured the skin around the eyes and Walker grew petrified as Malcolm's face emerged from the dark. Malcolm crouched low in the corner, seething like an animal, his naked skin shocked white with ash. Their line of vision connected in the mirror across the room and Walker froze in his bed, unable to move. Malcolm remained in the corner, oscillating his limbs as though ready to attack, clutching the same beveled dagger he had wielded in the dream. Walker could no longer tell if he was awake or asleep, but he knew that if he did not break from his paralysis and run for his life, the demonic aberration that appeared to him as his son was going to kill him. He struggled to toss back the blankets and fell to the floor with a thud. Malcolm remained in the mirror like a static, glitching still-life as Walker crawled past him, then rose to his feet and ran for the door.

The bathroom light shone into the hall, water ran from the faucet. Walker forced a dry swallow in his throat and whipped around, scowling behind him, but nobody followed. Trembling, he pushed the bathroom door open a couple of inches before it swung open from inside. "Didn't see you there, Dad," said Malcolm. He stood at the sink, using a wire brush to work the crimson stains from the front of his suit. When Walker gazed upon his son, he saw the brush as the knife from the dream and the burgundy tint of wine appeared to him as blood. Even the foam lathered from the baking soda translated into white ash crawling up his forearms to each elbow, same as the demon lurching in his room only a moment before.

The wet shirt was draped over the porcelain sink. Malcolm's pectorals were split by a lick of hair, his stomach and chest bare above the belt of his trousers. "You okay, Pa?" he mouthed. "I was trying to be quiet, thought you were asleep. What're you doing up?" Malcolm was not sure whether or not his father had heard him, so he repeated the question a second time. Walker staggered back, ripped apart by disbelief. He leered back down the hall, where he had seen his son crouching in the corner of his bedroom with a knife, then back to the bathroom, where Malcolm stood plain as day. He backed away from the bathroom, unsure and afraid, holding out his hands to shield himself as Malcolm came into the hall. Walker tried warning him to stay away, but the chords in his throat wrested together and struck him mute, so he gasped silently in horror.

Malcolm moved slowly toward him, asking if he was all right. Walker emitted a wounded sort of howl, an awful noise Malcolm had never heard before in his life. "Calm down," he consoled him. "It's okay, try and breathe." Malcolm's forearms dripped with white foam and he still had the wire brush in his right hand. Walker fixated on it, pointing, trying his best to scream. Walker struck out and shoved Malcolm away, continuing to back himself toward the head of the hall. Malcolm saw the trail of rain and wine his shirt had left as Walker set his bare heel down in it on the edge of the stairs. He lunged forth, reaching out to catch his father, but his hands closed on thin air as Walker crashed backward down the flight of stairs.

Outside on the stage, an electric crunch rang from an amplifier. Jordan held a low chord that vibrated his guts and turned to feedback through the speakers. When the heavy crash shook inside the house, Jordan dropped his guitar with a discordant clang, jumped off the stage, and ran through the crowd, shoving people aside as he ran up the porch and through the kitchen. He came to a stop at the foot of the stairs, where his father's body lay contorted in a heap. Jordan held his fingers to the side of Walker's neck, looking for a sign of life, and when he didn't feel a pulse knock back against his fingers, he leaned over his father's motionless body and looked up the stairwell at his brother sprawled out on his stomach, arms reached out in front of him. Malcolm and Jordan both laid there in a moment of quiet with Walker's corpse, each hoping they were at the apex of some nightmare from which they could still wake.

EIGHTEEN

The town of Carrollton had seen better days. The meager community, poised as it was on a difficult passage of the Ozarks plateau, once grew in multitudes—cattle was bred and fed, building financed, iron smithed, grocers and saloons traded in wares of necessity and vice. The hearts of the townsfolk broke when mothers watched their sons leave in equal droves for Rebel and Union camps. Neighbors that had been kind and dependent on each other for generations bickered and fought, families turned on one another. Frigid relations became permanent when boys from either side did not return from the fight. They did their best to persevere, but in the matter of a year, no more than two, Carrollton was destitute, a degradation from which it would never recover.

The war had taken a pernicious toll, undoubtedly, but a new scourge was upon them. The Confederate defeat at Prairie Grove that past December saw the nearby counties soaked in blood. Thousands dead, some local boys, others from as far away as Ohio and New York, fallen by each other's side as northwestern Arkansas fell to the Union. As word spread, morale was decimated, and a dread swept through the countryside worse than any disease. Confederate troops retreated back to Little Rock with their dead in tow, the force of life choked from each pallid, miserable face, while at the same time the Union moved their dead, treated their wounded, and restocked food and munitions from cracker lines in Missouri. It was a bitter winter out in the elements and any movement was slow. The dead were mourned and forgotten, the sick carried themselves once more, and eventually food, water, and rest enlivened the men enough to march east. General Blunt was bent on maximizing the gains of such a decisive victory. As locals and broadsheet headlines speculated, he planned to drive his men across the north of the state until they sat outside fortified Confederate positions across the Mississippi.

First, Blunt needed to reinforce and expand his corps of troops. After food and medicine came down the resupply, General Herron led an army of twenty thousand Union soldiers to set up camp on the outskirts of Carrollton, and their presence threw the town into immediate chaos. Fights plagued the local taverns so many nights that those who did not close their doors for good imposed curfews and hired private security. Quarrels born in those late hours saw their resolution in the dark and mudded streets. Pistols were easily drawn and fired, leaving corpses to bloat in the sun until they were dragged from sight and thrown in a pit behind the cemetery.

Tavern owner Jed Turrion was found in the alley behind his bar, shot through with a reckless spray of bullets, appearing to certain citizens of stature that he had been murdered for sport and nothing more. Not two weeks later, Mary Edin, a widowed mother of three, was gang raped by four Union soldiers on the very table where she served her children dinner and still set out a plate for her slain husband. The shame led her to hang herself from the gable of her one-room home as her three bright-eyed children watched from below. More women were beaten and raped. Carrollton's only bank was raided and burned to the ground, the body of its financier, John H. Faraday, found in the rubble. Finally, a group assembled in secret to decide what was to be done.

The meeting was called by a young smith named Andridge Sampson who operated one of the most frequented shops on the east edge of town. Andridge knew the widow Edin and her late husband well. His smithery was credited to in times of need by the generous Mr. Faraday and Andridge kept the profits he had earned in his bank, all of it now gone.

In '61, Andridge caught a bullet in his thigh at Wilson's Creek and was discharged with a shattered femur. He relocated to Carrollton at the behest of his friend, Benjamin Dunn, who suggested the sleepy plateau might be a place to live out his days in peace. Some businesses had continued to thrive in Carrollton, despite the war—smithing, milling peter, caskets and burial, the Lord. He formed a partnership with Ben and the Dunn-Sampson Blacksmithing Company was born. Andridge had been content to keep his head low and work, put the horrors of the past behind him, but now the northern barbarians were again at his doorstep and he could ignore them no longer. At night his mended wound ached and his mind flashed red with their unending trail of dead. He knew in his heart that there would be no peace until they were forced to leave. He convened the first meeting of concerned townsfolk, personally offering his hand to kill as many of those out-of-control scoundrels as he could.

Andridge assessed the grim faces gathered in the lanterns of Shackle Steven's boarded-up saloon. "We have got to be smart," Andridge began. "Those boys re-upped on guns, they been sitting around in camp, waiting on marching orders, itching for a fight. We're outmanned and outgunned a hundred to one, no question in that. If we run up in that camp rifles drawn, as some of you have suggested," he glared around accusingly, "you can say so long to everyone here in this room and those loved ones left at home soon thereafter. Those left earn the distinct honor of burying those quick to the gun and witnessing this town slide further into the mouth of hell."

Though Andridge chaired the meeting, three brothers named Martrue held the most influence over the group of twenty. The oldest Martrue, Andrew J., had a thin face sobered by violence. He squatted on a crate, sleeves rolled to his elbows, and did the talking for his brothers. "These are our families. We're tasked with protecting our wives and children, shops and businesses, our homes," he said. "I have lost," he paused to correct himself, "we have all lost a great deal to these invaders. I am not about to let them do as they like and destroy what's ours without consequence. We live here, they're passing through. I say we help them on their way, whether they like it or not."

"How do you suggest we do that?" Andridge asked.

"As you said, our force is small, but we know the land better than they do. We'll remain hidden, hit them when they are weakest, then scatter," Andrew said, confident.

While the assembly grumbled, Andridge meditated on actualizing such a plan. Then his hair stood on end and the muscles in his back straightened with the energy of a promising idea. "There is a train that hauls sulfur and salt from the mines, same train that brings in the ore we order at the shop. A federal car makes the trip from St. Louis twice a month. I saw them out there a few weeks ago, loading their wagons with supplies. The peter yield was low this year and demand is high, which means they have no gunpowder. Haven't seen them out there since, bet they're about due for another shipment."

Excited, the group grew to a roar. They had the place, now all they needed was a plan. "There's a depot thirty miles east, by the waypost at mile one twenty-two," Andridge continued. "It's secluded. There's a holler nearby, heavy cover that leads right up to the road." The precision of the plan burned cool in Andridge's mind as he saw it unfold. "I'll find out when that next haul of theirs comes in while you Martrues get a lead on guns and more men. Lord knows we'll need 'em."

Andrew Martrue conversed closely with his brothers and each looked back up with a fervent nod. "Thar's a militia over the border led by the Cader clan," Andrew told the group. "They run with bushwhackers in the river lands. Mean bastards, but fit to take any chance on hittin' Yanks, especially a regiment that ain't fixing to leave so soon. If it's guns and men we need, they's got plenty of both."

Andridge rose from his chair and convened with Andrew Martrue in the middle of the tavern floor, wrapping their arms around each other in a show of camaraderie that uplifted beleaguered spirits and reassured the members of their new militia. The rest of the group cheered and hugged, but Andridge was quick to scorn their ruckus and remind them to lower their voices to a whisper. They were still under enemy occupation, and a word spoken about what occurred there that night, he told them, would result in death. One by one, they filed out the back door into the alley and returned to their homes under cover of darkness, eager for the coming fight.

The slick black manes of the Caders shined down the hide-stitched backs of their leather vests, each stiff with seams of shotgun shells, a sheathed hatchet, and an Arkansas Toothpick—a giant, brass-handled Bowie knife each of them had strapped above the hip. They had the look of men tanned by hellfire, hardened from navigating the inhospitable layers of the underworld. Halbert Cader had a chaos of scars cut into the cracked and hardened skin of his forehead. His brother, Dell Cader, bore the lightened patch of a healed bullet hole that had sung straight through the fat in his cheek and out the other side. They greeted Andridge, but said little else past introducing the haggard members of their clan. With allegiances confirmed, they packed their horses, checked their arms, and began the ride out of Carrollton.

Two sisters rode second command to the brothers, storied bushwhackers whose reputations preceded them. Macy and Lacy Jane Pearl had survived alone when their father and brothers went off to fight, watching over young ones and keeping the sprawling acreage of their Missouri homestead from being ransacked by the Union or overrun by thieves.

The group rode through morning and by late afternoon had scouted the surrounding area and found a spot to ready the assault. Andridge rode ahead into the holler, crouching low to the back of his horse so as not be seen. Even though the troops would not arrive for another three hours, they spoke with hushed voices, stayed in the trees away from clearings, and took every precaution not to be seen. Three miles from the depot, the heavy tree cover opened upon a massive field overgrown with long grass and wild flowers, hemmed at every side by impenetrable forest. The Union soldiers would come through on their way to the depot and, upon returning, would journey into the wide open grove, slowed by their heavy wagons. Andridge and the militia would be there, lying in wait. They planned to take tree cover at the farthest end of the field. After the brigade passed, they would move into position, spread between the east edge of the field and the road.

Andridge took the youngest Martrue and rode out to scout the depot. They left their horses hidden in a shallow bank and crept to the crest of the ridgeline. "Keep your eye low," he instructed the boy. "What do you see?"

"A sea of blue," he said. "Not as many guns as we suspected."

"Good, that means they're still low on ammunition."

The boy realized the purpose of the shipment that the soldiers were busy unloading from the train. Andridge crouched next to him and did his best to estimate their progress. It was unusual for them to send seventy, eighty men for this type of job, Andridge thought. He worried they suspected an attack, but hoped that the sheer number of troops was evidence of how vulnerable they felt being temporarily underarmed. In addition to gunpowder, the soldiers hauled crates of potatoes, onions, and canned beans, clothing, campware, shovels, rakes, picks, and axes. They moved crates of tobacco and booze and boxes marked with white crosses full of medical supplies. Andridge's mind raced. By the look of it, they were loading in supplies to last out the winter. They could have even been planning to turn their camp into a full-time settlement.

The wagons sagged through the mud as they clamored back from the depot. After being on the trail that led back to Carrollton for a few hours, the Union corps commander was distracted by a miraculous vision. The Pearl sisters rode out on two mares, white as snow, their ruffled dresses, one tan, the other red, both crimped in white. In truth, these were the only dresses the girls had ever owned and they thought it amusing to put them to such use. Their hair was streaked blonde and curled proper, held in place with pristine silk bows. The march slowed to a crawl, the commander charmed.

"Where are you fine ladies off to?" he called. "Surely, you're not riding out here all by your lonesome?"

"We're not lonesome, we have each other," said Macy. They eked out girlish laughs and acted shy, the way they thought weak women were supposed to act.

"We were out for an afternoon lesson, but seem to have gotten separated from the rest of the group," Lacy Jane told the commander.

"It's not safe out here, misses, especially for women of pedigree such as yourselves," he cautioned. "Which direction you headed?"

Macy Pearl pointed her gloved hand up the road. "We came from over there, I think. Though I'm afraid we might have lost our way," she said, doing her best to sound wayward and wounded.

"Well say, if that ain't the direction we're marching in ourselves. You'll ride the rest of the way with us, up here with me at the helm." The commander grinned with bravado and postured his chest, heaving under blue wool, interlocking gold slips, and brass buttons.

The men in the back stared at the veil of surrounding brush and kicked their feet in the dirt, annoyed by the arduousness of their task and more so that they had come to a stop. They smoked tobacco and took out their knives to whittle branches and pry holes in the cantles of their saddles. The sky was broad and hazy with heat, the farther it stretched the lower it sagged across miles of rolling hills. When the march got moving again, the girls rode up front aside the commander. It was all they could do not to laugh, aware of how ridiculous they looked, a couple of killers dolled up in bows and Sunday dresses. As they got closer to the grove, though, they grew gravely serious, exchanging only looks of kinship and blood. The soldiers had taken the bait.

A dirt path opened beneath a break in the trees. The Pearl sisters counted with even nods of their heads, mouthing in silence— *one, two, three.* Wrought whips cracked on hide and they held on as their young mares screamed into the wind, bounding toward dense pine. The commander was muddled with surprise and was left with no time to react before a wall of bullets sprayed from invisible positions in the trees. He opened his mouth to yell, but a bullet trained by Andrew Martrue flew straighter than truth into the commander's throat and out the back of his skull, exploding a gore of sinew and fat across the faces of the staff and gunnery sergeants who sat abreast their horses behind him.

Andridge and Andrew darted up, each flanked by ten men. Mounted Union troops realized that their ranking officer was dead and the staff sergeant called for the men to take cover from the gunfire. Andridge closed ground and the bluecoats tasked with accompanying the wagons fled on foot. The Caders rode fast through meadow grass, making a game of getting as close as possible to their targets before striking them down. They slowed within arm's reach of the soldiers, young and terrified, not sure whether they wanted to flee and live or stay and die, leering in horror at grizzled men cut from stone, purified by loss, clenching their teeth in proud, maniacal smiles as they drove the dull blades of their axes into the necks and backs of the young soldiers, quartering flesh above the shoulder, before circling back around to slit their throats. Huge chunks of meat fell between the feet of the horses. Those who tried to run staggered a few steps and bled out in the flowers.

Andridge and Andrew Martrue flanked both columns of troops and met at the back end of the march. The hail of fire grew closer, spooking untethered horses that bucked and took off sprinting through clouds of dust. The field was alive with battle, animosity and retribution drudged up and hurled forth with unrelenting brutality. Losing a battle was not as bad a prospect as having the victors remain in their towns and live among their families as occupiers. They called out the names of their raped daughters, sisters, and wives, kin laid by poverty, starvation, and suicide, invoking their dead as they shot and cut their way through the line.

A person who killed out of vengeance was seldom stopped. They reaped whatever moved, spreading death like gospel. Colts were pressed hard under shelves of ribs and the sharp bones of temples, dropping new bodies on top of old ones. Wagons were staggered across the field on their sides, strewing crates of food and supplies, split barrels of gunpowder tethered to the weight of dead horses. Equine eyes frozen a cloudy white, ribs peppered with buckshot, stomach sacks slid steaming in the dirt. Soldiers still alive lay wounded, their blood seeping into the soil. Downed rebels rolled in the grass clutching holes in their limbs, screaming in agony, while a determined few crawled on their elbows toward any nearby enemy still breathing to choke the life out of them.

Andridge Sampson lay among the dying. A shot had ripped into his side and the force of the bullet knocked him clear off his horse. He hit the ground, trapped in a blurry cloud of swift-moving shapes. Andridge spread out on his back and stared straight into the sun.

Weakened by the bullet, the weight of his body lessened. He felt as though he was being consolidated, reduced to his most basic elements and flattened into one dimension, thin as paper and lighter than air. His perception sifted free from its enclosure in the skull and he was able to see without eyes. Andridge floated above the tops of the trees and saw his own body, gun slung at his hip, hat knocked from his head, clothes soiled with his and other men's blood. A trail of clear blue light leaked from the site of his wound, a mysterious vapor flowing out of him. His purview kept widening until it included the site of the massacre and the entire grove, dead bodies heaped in their final resting places, burned into the earth like coal.

While looking over the field, Andridge became aware that he was moving farther away, expanding in size but somehow growing lighter and less dense, like the sun itself. Andridge maneuvered away from the ground and turned to face the sky. The hollow portal of the sun took control of him and blinded him with its absolute power, enveloping him in a trance. Any consciousness that reflected his self was lost. The sun spoke in a language that had always been there, vibrating in ancient trees and animal ancestors, consecrated in feather, bone, and brain, resonating in waves of eternal memory. An understanding of God was born throughout his circuitry and filled Andridge as he lifted up and spread throughout the sky.

Andridge Sampson's entire being was stretched and illumined, and the awareness he had of himself transformed from the exterior, which had spread to almost nothing, to the interior, where he was pregnant with a golden egg split at the middle by a pervasive crack. He traveled through the crack into the center, where there were two eggs, the two halves married at the site of fracture. The crack along the surface opened like a seam and the two wholes came back together in a brilliant circle that vanished once unified with the void of the sun. Then he began to fall, hurled into an ever-widening crevice that grew into more elaborate gulfs and chasms. Andridge continued falling through deeper cracks of time and space until he sped through a barrier of cloud and the earth once again became visible, sprouting like a weed from the abyss.

Andridge awoke beneath the considered gaze of a young girl. Weakness decimated his attempts to move or speak. He was tucked beneath a blanket in a comfortable bed in a clean, well-kept house. Daylight glowed through the blind drawn over the only window. He folded back the covers and basked in the relief of fresh air on his skin. Regaining his senses overwhelmed him at first. Weakness sapped his muscles, stiffness spread to the rigid tips of his toes. A high-pitched ringing pierced the drum of his inner ear, when he flexed his jaw the room went mute. His tongue flopped foreign in his mouth, and he still could barely hear past his own breathing.

The girl moved around the room then approached the bedside with water. She raised the rim of the glass and wetted the closed seam of Andridge's lips until they opened enough for her to drip the water into his mouth. His whole body decompressed with relief. Even though she had grown accustomed to a gray, ravaged face cut up and grown over with a dark beard, she leaned close and studied him as if for the first time, amazed he had woken. Softly, Andridge asked who she was.

"Pria Fairchild. My family owns this cottage. You were wounded in an awful fight." She held back the opaque curtain and pointed. "Back there, in the grove beyond those woods. Many others were killed, you were lucky to have survived. Robert and I— Robbie's my little nephew—we heard the fighting and hid in the dirt cellar, figuring it was a raid. We live here just the two of us, most of our family is gone. Our distant uncle checks in on us from time to time, but mostly it's Robbie and I getting by."

She assisted Andridge in taking a few sips of water, then smoothed the front of her dress and repositioned herself on the edge of the bed. "I remember that night we found you, there was a terrible rain. A few hours passed and we hadn't heard gunfire, so we peeked out to take a look. Night had fallen and the storm was still railing. Robbie thought we couldn't keep a torch lit in such a coming down, and we didn't want to be found, so we walked out there in the dark. Our clothes were soaked and the rain fell in big drops from our lashes. I reckon it a blessing we ventured all that way, undetected."

She shook her head and averted her eyes. "How awful, what we found there. Men and horses, all shot dead. It was like a graveyard had been dug up. The rain kept scavengers away and washed all that blood down in the soil. We stayed in the trees for a long while, until we knew for sure nobody was coming back. When we were confident we were out there alone, we walked among the bodies—shot up, twisted, and hacked—a man had died on his knees with his hands together, praying face down in the mud. Robbie heard you crying, but we couldn't tell where it was coming from. When we passed back a second time, we found you."

The massacre began to come back to Andridge in vague, remote impressions. His heart raced with panic, his legs itched, his sweat was like needles on his skin. He struggled to get up but fell back on the mattress, coughing in his pillow. Pria tended to him and asked Andridge what was wrong.

"Survivors," Andridge managed to cough out. "They're bound to have made it back to camp in Carrollton by now. We're not safe here, they're going to come for us." He sat up again, looking around, saying, "It's not safe," over and over.

"Please, mister, ain't nobody coming," Pria reasoned. "We're all right here, I promise you." Her consolations calmed Andridge. Besides, he did not possess the energy to fight her.

Pria changed the cold cloth on his head. Andridge's disorientation gave way to profound confusion. Had no one survived the attack? Perhaps word had not yet made it back to Carrollton? He mumbled bits and pieces of such inquiries to himself and then asked Pria what had happened.

"Eventually, I read it in the paper," she told him. "Fourteen Carrollton militiamen dead, fifty-three Yankees. Near as many as were out there that day, according to the paper. A few survived. They came back to pick through all that could be salvaged, but nobody came here."

"Read it in a newspaper? News travels fast, I reckon."

Pria covered her laugh out of courtesy. "That news-sheet's well past a month old, mister. I'm sure you don't remember, but you were in a sick sleep, nothing was going to wake you. You been in that bed for exactly forty-nine days. That is why I am so taken with surprise—and joy, of course—that you woke this morning. I prayed every day right by this bed that you should remain with us. Oh, how my prayers came true! I told the Lord, I said you were not ready to go, you had a task of great importance to fulfill, and that, His will permitting, you would rise again and walk the earth for a long time to come."

The water stayed down so Andridge asked Pria for a small amount of food. She returned with a basket and threw back the napkin to reveal a fresh-baked blueberry pie. She carefully cut a slice, then used the knife to crumble it onto a small plate that she held in front of Andridge.

"There you go," she said. "You need the sugar."

The sweetness of the berries electrified his senses and called him back to life. He sat with his back to the wall and a virulent pain traveled down his throat and caught fire in the right side of his hip when he swallowed. Once he recovered from the shock, he recalled falling from his horse, the realization that he had been shot coming later. He spread a palm across his hipbone. "I was shot here," he said. "Must've knocked my head when I fell." He pulled back the blanket and inspected the wound. Pria had it all sewn up and the stitches were in the midst of being forced out of the skin.

"This one could have laid me down for good, but you saved me, Pria. I'll never know how to thank you," Andridge said.

"You don't have to, mister." She paused and fluttered her eyes before looking back at him. "You know, it's silly, but I have yet to learn your name."

"It's Andridge," he told her. "Andridge Sampson."

"I like that," said Pria. "I had been referring to you simply as our guest. Nice to put a name with the face."

Andridge smiled warmly. "Were you able to recover the bullet?"

"That was the easy part. As I said before, you were in a dead sleep, so you didn't make so much as a fuss about it," Pria explained. She grew grim and fiddled the ring on her thin finger before placing her palm on top of his, cupping the tender skin around the healing scar. "That was not so much my concern, see. I thought you were hurt from the bullet alone, but when I removed it, your condition worsened. I worried you'd infected, but it wasn't just fever. After examining you for near three whole weeks, I realized there was something else. I don't quite know how to say this—I found something in your abdomen. A blockage, it was quite serious."

Andridge listened intently. The room, once comforting to him, now held him hostage with anticipation and forced him to abide by the restraint in Pria's voice.

She wrinkled her brow and considered how to proceed. "I had to cut you open a second time," she said. "One across your belly, the second a vertical cut from the first one all the way down to your groin. Thankfully, Robbie and I recovered a medical kit from one of those wagons we found in the field."

"How'd you know to do that?" asked Andridge, confused how a girl so young could have acquired even a basic understanding of surgery.

"I used to work on the horses with father when this was still a farm," she said, holding back the listless, bitter sting of longing.

He had not thought of it until then, but Andridge considered how he registered no feeling below his pelvis. In a growing panic, he inspected the sight of the surgery Pria had performed. He wanted to scream. Nausea spread from the weak vestiges of his body. He had no choice but to listen.

"The cuts were deep, below the tissue. You have to understand, you were unresponsive for weeks. You could not eat or drink, your body was beginning to shut down. I proffered a guess that removing the protrusion from your stomach was going to save your life. It was the only option left to take," Pria said.

She sprung from the bedside and left the room. Andridge could hear her talking to someone in the hall, but he could not make out what was being said. After a few minutes, she returned. Pria held open the door and young Robert came in, freckled black hair and worn overalls, gently cradling a swaddling cloth. He stepped to the bed and loosened the thick white fabric to reveal two pure, unimaginable faces, day breaking through thinly opened eyelids, round cheeks flushed red, two identical licks of hair swirling the backs of soft, infant heads.

"I swear it's a miracle, Mister Andridge," said Pria, standing beside Robbie. "I don't have an explanation for how this could have happened, never would I have thought I would be charged with something so perplexing and so downright miraculous." She received the babies from Robbie and lowered them into Andridge's grasp. He cradled them and gently held their heads on his chest. "Mister Andridge, sir, I would like to introduce you to your sons," said Pria. "Twins, in fact."

NINETEEN

ANDRIDGE PREPARED HIS CABIN for a long period of rest. He shot his goat and set his chickens free, sure the animals would not survive the coming sleep. He toiled behind the cabin through a mess of tools and gas cans, transmissions, and radiator parts rusted among the weeds. He made his way to the propane tank, reached through the towering briars, and wrenched the valve closed.

The corner of the notched fence marked their boundary from the meadow that cascaded down into Reed's Gap. Cob peered down into the valley from the warped steel saddle of a decommissioned tractor. Eyes closed, a look of harmonious consideration relaxed the muscles in his face as he attuned to the living conversation of plants, animals, people, and the occasional passage of invisible bodies. A moment before, Cob had caressed the bone cleft between the eyes of the goat, communing him a blessing which the goat commiserated, letting Cob know just how tired he had grown, assuring him he was ready to go. "It looks like both of us are going to sleep then, old friend," Cob told the goat. He brushed his palm on the knobs of the goat's spine before Andridge came over with the Springfield.

Inside the cabin, Cob unplugged the gas pilot for the stove and joined Andridge in dry-stocking the kitchen and shuttering the windows, which drew their quarters in the resolute darkness to which they were accustomed. They came together in front of the fireplace, taking their time removing the ritual objects, charts, and photographs of the Bayne family, placing them in a cardboard box that Andridge stored in a crawlspace in the wall.

"It is done," said Cob. "Malcolm actually manifested as the slayer. No conduit, no catalyst to help him along. The boy has a strong will. Jordan was an obvious firebrand all those years, but with Malcolm, I didn't know how it was going to unfold."

"There was less to work with this time," Andridge said. "The less the spirit was able to achieve direct influence, the more gradually it bent them to its will. In many ways, it was the most pure cycle we have seen yet." Andridge thought about what he had just said. "I wonder if this means that the myth is changing, progressing in some way. We have seen it grow from simple hatred into more complex forms, as though the myth is perfecting itself."

"It's thinking," said Cob. He finished packing the last of their belongings and locked the doors. "Do you think it still matters?" he asked Grieves. "I look out there, I am not sure it is as effective as it once was. I can no longer see the effects. There used to be a lull, a calm, a period of pacification as a result of the sacrifice. Then it would start all over again. You say the myth is growing more abstract, more pure, less a product of baser emotions, but I only see the world moving toward disorder."

"There are more people on Earth than ever before and they are distracting themselves from what is required in order for them to survive," said Andridge. "The web of satellites and computers, these intelligent phones, highways, cars, and garbage everywhere, it is so much that I cannot even think as I used to. I used to be able to hear thoughts, now they are all scrambled. I find it unpleasant and loud, but their desperation is most deafening. Pretty soon, no orchestration of ours will matter. There are other watchers with responsibilities greater than our own. Greater gods begin and end worlds at a whim, when they turn over or are roused from their slumber by a terrible dream. At some point, no amount of blood will satisfy."

The time had come to part. Cob was flushed with immense relief, allowing the fatigue that had built up over a long wakefulness to wash over him. Neither Andridge nor Cob were ones for sentiment, so Cob stood at the entrance to his bedroom and smiled, a gesture Andridge returned with a bow of his head. He watched as Cob's tan suit sank into the depthless dark of his room. He pushed the door closed and snapped shut the lock, sealing him into his hermetic chamber until the next time they were required. Andridge sat in his old rocker and lit his favorite cigar. He sucked in the fire from the flare of two matches until a ribbon of smoke dovetailed in front of him. Andridge shook out the matches, turned up a slat on the window blind, and cast his tired eyes upon the night sky.

A spectral aura permeated the deep wood. Jordan rustled through brush, mind not so much clear as void. He had left the scene at the house, the consoling and weeping awe. With Malcolm in shock, Elizabeth and her mother made arrangements for the body. He assumed they had moved him by now. Minutes were hours that bore tortuous weight. To have stayed would have meant a grief without end, so Jordan slipped out the back and walked into the trees. First he staggered aimless and half-hearted, but soon he found his step and the way appeared before him.

Jordan came to the center of that lowly glow. With the field before him, he was confounded by what he saw. The night he and Malcolm had found their way out there, the grove was wild and overgrown. Now it was cut clear to the stands of trees that rose in each direction. The call of the culling had been answered. Jordan carved a path across open ground to the pond beneath the shadow of the elm. Where moonlight parted the water, a set of stairs descended into the depths of the earth.

ACKNOWLEDGMENTS

I would like to thank my editor and brother-in-arms, Guy Intoci, for his vision and hard work in bringing this book to print, as well as Michelle Dotter, Michael Seidlinger, Steven Gillis, Dan Wickett, and the entire Dzanc Books team for all they do for independent literature. My agent Lukas Ortiz at the Philip G. Spitzer Literary Agency, for his unwavering support for this book and my career. Jonathan Evison, for being an early reader, mentor, and friend, and for the many late-night writing sessions, beer, and ping-pong matches out at the cabin on the Olympic Peninsula, where sections of this book were written. Peter Geye, Kristen Millares Young, and Harry Kirchner, who read early drafts and provided thoughtful notes that greatly improved the book. I would also like to thank Harry for his friendship and partnership in Phalos Editions, the imprint we were fortunate enough to found and operate together until it found a new, happy home. Max Kirchner, the best friend and screenwriting partner anyone could ever hope for. Jenn Risko at Shelf Awareness for her smart, generous, and gracious years of friendship.

Aaron, Rhyan, and Rohan Augustus Talwar, my closest friends and extended family. My actual family: Rick, Debra, Brett, Claudine, Liz, Evan, and Sara, endless love to you all. Lastly, my wife, Rachel Dorothy Blowen. Scales of justice and fairness, cosmic skunk, warrior of Ukok and Astarte, welder, sculptor, mystic, carrier of the light. Thank you, love, for making this life so beautiful.

In no particular order, I would also like to thank: Richard Hugo House, Cheap Beer & Prose, APRIL, Seattle Fiction Federation, Dock Street Salon, Lit Fix, Lit Crawl, Seattle7Writers, Doe Bay Resort on Orcas Island, Elliot Bay Book Company, Third Place Books, University Bookstore, Phinney Books, Village Books, Powell's Books, Publishers Group West (PGW), David Dahl, Cindy Heidemann, Kevin Votel, Gary Lothian, Kathi Kirby, Larry Olson, Marilyn Dahl, Paul Gjording, Kris Meyer, Craig Young, Andre Dubus III, Garth Stein, Jennie Shortridge, Donald Ray Pollock, Brian Evenson, Benjamin Percy, Nickolas Butler, Tim Horvath, Sean Beaudoin, Joshua Mohr, James Greer, Lidia Yuknavitch, Kate Lebo, Sam Ligon, Brian Young, Ian Denning, Mia Lipman, Dane Bahr, Jeanine Walker, Robert P. Kaye, Christine Texiera, Jill Owens, Elissa Washuta, Matt Revert, Tyson Cornell, Pat Walsh, Tobias Carroll, Matthew Simmons, Paul Constant, Karen Maeda Allman, Emily Adams, Paul Hanson, Tom Nissley, Lindsey, David, and Delilah Joan Stone, Ben Yuse, Carolyn Beagan, Jacquelyn and Dan Benson, Jared and Erin Millson, Kyle and Sara Haakenson, Andrew Rea, Allison MacManus, Ashley Nelson, Erin Bradt, Ian Ciesla, Patski Lonergan, Deborah Farrell, Chris Jessick, Mike Jessick, Chris Conant, Neil Mooney, Andrew Legendre, John Carroll, Laura Keating, Benjamin Van Pelt, and all the writers, artists, readers, and booksellers who keep the dream alive.